JEB STUART

By *Lena Y. de Grummond*
and *Lynn de Grummond Delaune*

ILLUSTRATED BY A. CHRIS SIMON

PELICAN PUBLISHING COMPANY

Gretna 1979

85-1301

JEB STUART

To Dick,
a beloved husband and dear son-in-law,
who shares the military heritage of Jeb Stuart.

CONTENTS

INTRODUCTION

"HERE he comes! Here comes Jeb Stuart!"

The long line of ragged gray infantrymen resting along the roadside pulled themselves up for a better look. People always wanted a better look at Jeb Stuart.

He sat on his beautiful horse—and his horses were always beautiful—as though he were part of it. As Jeb galloped, his long gray cape blew back. Its brilliant scarlet lining billowed in the wind. One side of his wide-brimmed gray hat was fastened up, giving a yet more dashing touch to its appearance. From it a long graceful plume waved gaily. His snowy gauntlets, his fine uniform with its brass and leather gleaming with reflected light, his full flowing beard turning golden red where the sun touched it—all made him look the part of his nickname—"the joyous cavalier." He rode to battle singing. This was as much a part of him as the saber in his hand. All these characteristics, combined with his genius as a leader of cavalry and his great personal bravery, contributed to his place in history and made him a legend while he lived. He was beloved and celebrated among his compatriots and fellows-at-arms in a way few have been.

Chapter I.

A FIGHTER
FROM THE START

JEB's ancestors on both sides had illustrious records of public service. They had often served as governors and legislators and had been men of wealth and influence. In time of war they had distinguished themselves as valiant soldiers.

Jeb's father, Archibald Stuart, continued this record of public service. He represented Patrick County in the Virginia Assembly for many years and also was a member of the federal Congress for a time. He served as an officer in the United States Army in the War of 1812. Besides being a noted orator, Mr. Stuart was renowned for his social grace, his wit and charm. At least some of Jeb's dash and gaiety must have come from his father. And both he and his father were noted for their voices. Mr. Stuart was spoken of as having "a fine singing voice," and of course the qualities of his son's voice, in command or song, were famous. Archibald Stuart was a handsome, vigorous man. It was said that few men in public life in Virginia have been so loved.

He was not, however, a very good businessman. Perhaps he was too easygoing and convivial. At any rate, it seems that much of Jeb's strong moral fiber, his piety, and his overwhelming devotion to duty came to him from his mother, Elizabeth Pannill Letcher. It was she, who gave him the firm and simple religious training that was always an important force in his life. She also, when he was twelve years old, asked an oath of him never to touch liquor, and he never did, refusing it even to relieve the suffering of the wound that killed him.

Into the household established by these two, Elizabeth Pannill Letcher and Archibald Stuart, at Laurel Hill in Virginia, James Ewell Brown Stuart—in later years his initials gave him his famous nickname—was born on February 6, 1833. He was the seventh of their eleven children, and their youngest son.

From early boyhood he was vigorous and hardy. An older brother, William Alexander, tells of an encounter he and young James had with some hornets that shows other characteristics of the boy. One day when William Alexander was about fifteen and James about nine, the two boys noticed an unusually large hornets' nest in the branches of a big tree. It was about the size of a football, and they both thought it should come down. The question was—how? Its position was such that they couldn't knock it down by throwing sticks. At last they decided they'd have to climb the tree. They climbed closer and closer and then, just as they were almost close enough to go to work on it, out swarmed the hornets! William Alexander decided it wasn't worth that, dropped to the ground, and ran. James, however, kept right on going. All those stings didn't stop him. He hit the nest with his stick and dislodged it before he, too, jumped. William Alexander said later that this showed him that James had the makings of a fine soldier.

James was for the most part tutored at home until, at fifteen, he entered Emory and Henry College. He wanted to take the advanced Latin classes offered there and wrote one of his former tutors for a certificate to show he had completed the simpler courses which, he said, "you instilled into me partly by the mouth and partly by the rod." James liked Latin, which he considered an important part of his preparation for his future career in schoolteaching. His plan was changed, apparently quite suddenly. Archibald Stuart lost his seat in Congress to a Mr. H. T. Averett. Mr. Averett's first official act was to give the son of his opponent an appointment to West Point. So on July 1, 1850, when he was seventeen years old, James Ewell Brown Stuart became a cadet at the United States Military Academy.

At West Point Jeb, even though he was more interested in military than scholastic attainments, stood fairly high in his class. He was eighth in a class of seventy-one his first year and seventh in a class of sixty his second. During his last two years he dropped considerably lower and ended as thirteenth in the class of forty-six who survived. In the Stuart family there is a tradition that Jeb deliberately let his grades slide that last year. It seems that the cadets with the highest grades automatically went into the Corps of Engineers. Now Jeb preferred the cavalry, and so, they say, he let his class standing fall just low enough to make sure he would miss the engineers!

Though not among the very highest of his class, Jeb held the ranks of cadet, orderly, sergeant, and second captain during his cadet years, and these were achievements to be proud of. He also received a large number of demerits.

Most of these were for fighting, which he obviously loved. Even in those days, when a gentleman fought for his honor at what we today would consider the drop of a hat, Jeb Stuart got into scrapes more often than most. Once his father wrote him, "I have received your letter and much regret that you have been involved in another fighting scrape. My dear son, I can excuse more readily a fault of the sort you have committed, in which you maintained your character as a man of honor and courage, than almost any other. But I hope you will hereafter, as far as possible, avoid getting into difficulties in which such maintenance may be demanded at your hands."

While Jeb was at West Point, the commandant of the Military Academy was Brevet Lieutenant Colonel Robert E. Lee. George Washington Custis Lee, his son, was leading his class each year, just as his father had done before him.

Another schoolmate was Fitz Lee, a nephew of the commandant, who later became Stuart's companion-in-arms. Fitz Lee remembered that even then Stuart was noted for "a strict attention to his military duties, an erect, soldierly bearing, an immediate and almost thankful acceptance of a challenge from a cadet to fight . . . and a clear, metallic, ringing voice." Fitz Lee mentions Jeb's voice again. He says, "There was so much music in his voice, sounding like the trumpet of the Archangel."

At the academy James Ewell Brown Stuart was universally called "Beauty." Fitz Lee tells us something about this nickname. "However manly and soldierly in appearance he afterwards grew," he says, "in those days his comrades called him 'Beauty' to express their idea of his personal comeliness in inverse ratio to the compliment implied."

They called him "Beauty" because they thought he was anything but that!

Jeb Stuart apparently enjoyed his years at West Point. He said once of the academy, "If it could be grafted on Virginia soil I would consider it a paradise." He graduated in July 1854 and was made a brevet second lieutenant of the mounted rifles. His commission as a regular second lieutenant came on October 31, 1854.

Lieutenant Stuart's first assignment was with the mounted rifles serving in Texas. Because of a yellow fever epidemic in New Orleans, through which he had to pass, he did not arrive at Fort Clark until December 1854. Once with the regiment, he served on many small expeditions against the Apache and Comache Indians. These patrols traveled in the Trans-Pecos and Texas Panhandle areas, covering some of the most difficult terrain in the world. Here Lieutenant Stuart led groups of men, often completely out of touch with headquarters or other units for days on end, frequently short on water and food, and always subject to savage, though usually brief, encounters with the Indians. Under these conditions Jeb had many opportunities to develop his leadership ability and initiative.

One of these expeditions that Jeb liked to remember involved a steep Indian trail and a cannon. The patrol he was leading had been traveling over a rising tableland that was here rough, here smooth. Suddenly the advance guard came to an abrupt halt, finding themselves upon the crest of an enormous precipice. Directly in front of them the cliff dropped off a straight two thousand feet. On the other side of a broad valley rose a similar vertical wall of rock. There seemed no way into the valley. Yet as they looked again they saw there was. A very narrow Indian path carved in the solid rock zigzagged dangerously down the sheer face of the cliff. As the men began cautiously to edge their way down, one of the soldiers came up to Stuart. "Well, Leftenant," he said, "what you gwine to do with the cannon?"

"You stay up here," answered Stuart, "until I go down and pick out a road." Jeb said later that the last thing in the world he was looking for was a place to take the cannon down. What he really wanted to find at the bottom of that cliff was an order from Major Simonson saying he could abandon the cannon. No such order was waiting. So back he went up the trail.

"Unhitch the mules from the cannon, Jack," he ordered, "and start on down the path with them."

Then he turned to the captain of the ranger company that had been detailed to remain behind the artillery.

"Sir," he said, "with the help of some of your men I think we can get that cannon down. The major left no orders about it, so I cannot and will not forsake it."

"All right," said the captain.

"We'll unlimber the piece," said Stuart, "and if you, Captain, with twenty-five men, will start down in command of the limber, I'll take another twenty-five and take charge of the piece itself. Here is the route I'd suggest we take." With that Jeb pointed out to the other officer the path he had chosen. A few minutes later the captain and his men started down the cliffside carrying the detachable fore part of the gun carriage.

Then Lieutenant Stuart and his twenty-five men began the long, slow, dangerous descent with the heavy cannon piece itself. They tied it with lariat ropes and—heaving, shoving, pushing—lifted it over the huge rocks blocking the narrow path. Finally, with many a sigh of relief, they reached the bottom safely.

Astonishment reigned at the major's bivouac when, shortly before dark, Lieutenant Stuart and his men appeared *with* the cannon!

Major Simonsen had not left orders to abandon it at the top of the cliff because he had taken it for granted that that was the only thing that could be done. That night, as Stuart sat before the bivouac fires sipping his coffee, the major told him, "I certainly never expected to see you bring the artillery down that mountain. You deserve great credit for your success."

Such resourcefulness and determination did not go unnoticed in other quarters. In the spring of 1855, when the officers for the proud new 1st and 2nd Cavalry Regiments were announced, Lieutenant Stuart's name was on the list.

Chapter II.

INDIAN ENCOUNTER

THE 1st Cavalry Regiment, to which Lieutenant Stuart was assigned, was one of two new cavalry regiments organized by the Secretary of War, Mr. Jefferson Davis. Before this the U. S. Army had had mounted rifles—infantrymen who used their horses merely for transportation— and dragoons—heavy men on heavy horses who fought either on foot or on horseback. The two new cavalry regiments would be used for mounted combat only. The cavalrymen would be formed into fast, quick-moving units that could be used for scouting or shock tactics. Their arms would be the saber and pistol.

The officers for these two new units were very carefully selected. As it turned out, Mr. Secretary Davis chose for these officer corps men who were later to be among the most outstanding leaders on both sides in the Civil War. From this group came over thirty corps, division, and brigade commanders; five full generals of the Confederate Army; and two Union Army commanders. If Secretary Davis wished to create a *corps d'élite*, he succeeded.

On the third of March 1855, Lieutenant J. E. B. Stuart

was transferred to the 1st Cavalry Regiment and thus became a member of this elite group. He was ordered to Jefferson Barracks in St. Louis, where the new regiments were being whipped into shape. By August the 1st Cavalry was well enough organized to move to its new station in the Kansas Territory. Along with it went Second Lieutenant Stuart, acting as its regimental quartermaster.

Jeb may not have been too happy with this first assignment. After all, the task of caring for food and equipment probably did not seem as dashing, glamorous, or exciting a job as the broad-shouldered young cavalryman must have at first hoped for. It was a job that was to give him experience that would stand him in good stead later, however. Because of it he was probably one of the first men in the U. S. Army to learn first hand how to cope with all the problems involved in keeping a modern cavalry troop fed, supplied, and mounted.

Arriving in the Kansas Territory, the 1st Cavalry Regiment reported to Fort Leavenworth. The commandant of the fort was Colonel Philip St. George Cooke, a man who was to play an important part in young Stuart's life. Colonel Cooke had three daughters. Jeb must have met one of them, Flora, almost as soon as he arrived at Leavenworth, for by the time the regiment left for an expedition against the Indians some three weeks or so later, he and Flora were engaged. Tradition has it that he wooed and won the lady of his choice in only two weeks! Evidently he campaigned for her heart with all the dash, ardor, and vigor that characterized his campaigning in the field of light cavalry.

Though born in Missouri and graduated from a private school in Detroit, Flora shared with Jeb a tie with his well-loved state of Virginia. Her army family had originally come from there. They shared another interest, too. Flora was an excellent horsewoman, and she and her dashing young suitor must have enjoyed many horseback rides along the paths near Fort Leavenworth during their short courtship.

As soon as Jeb received Flora's acceptance, he wrote his father to ask his blessing upon the coming marriage. This was readily given. Only a few weeks later, however, while the 1st Cavalry was still out on its first expedition, Stuart received another message from home. This one bore quite different tidings—his beloved father was dead. Jeb's deep grief is very apparent in the letters of this time.

In November the troop came back to Fort Leavenworth. It had done no actual fighting, as the Indians had withdrawn to their mountain strongholds. Meanwhile Flora's father had been transferred to Fort Riley. As soon as possible after his return from the expedition, the eager young second lieutenant hurried over.

On November 14, 1855, at Fort Riley, Kansas, James Ewell Brown Stuart and Flora Cooke were married. Though women certainly lavished an unusual amount of praise and affection upon Stuart during his years as a hero of the Confederacy, and he obviously enjoyed their attentions, Flora Stuart was always the only woman in his life.

Jeb and Flora set up housekeeping in the rough quarters given them at Fort Leavenworth. It was only a frontier log hut, but Jeb made it ring with his songs and laughter. Only a month after their marriage they received some happy news—Second Lieutenant Stuart was made a first lieutenant on December 20, 1855—an unusually fast promotion.

During these early years of their marriage the young couple were often separated. Bloody conflict over its future

slave or free status shook the Kansas Territory, and the
1st Cavalry Regiment was often out on expeditions as it tried
to keep the peace.

Then, too, the Indian raids became increasingly worse.
Finally, in 1857, the 1st Cavalry took the field against them.
For weeks the regiment lived on the trail and engaged in a
number of skirmishes. The major encounter of the campaign
occurred when the regiment, under Colonel Sumner, came
suddenly upon three hundred Cheyenne Indians. What a
sight they made, gaudy with war paint and drawn up in a
long line of battle!

At once the six companies under Colonel Sumner formed
into a line. Quickly Jeb organized his company. Tense and
excited, he sat on his horse, waiting to shout out the order
for his men to charge. He expected to order them to gallop
forward with pistols drawn as the Indians were already
within gunshot. He lifted his eyebrows in surprise when he
heard Colonel Sumner's voice ring out with the command
"Draw *sabers!* Charge!" A terrific shout rose—the cavalry
troops spurred their mounts and the lines leaped forward!

Almost at once the Cheyennes turned in disorderly flight.
The blue-coated riders set out in swift pursuit. At first Jeb's
horse, Dan, was able to keep close to the fleeing Indians,
even though their ponies were much fresher. For five miles
Dan and his vigorous young rider were hot on their trail.
Then Dan tired. When Jeb saw that Dan was not going to
be able to keep up the pace, he leaped from the saddle.
Giving Dan's reins to someone else, he commandeered the
horse of a private, vaulted into the saddle, and galloped off.
Away they went, traveling at top speed. They soon caught
up with the other handful of cavalrymen who had been
able to stay close behind the Indians.

When Stuart reached the rear of the ragged Cheyenne line he found one of his fellow officers, Lomax, in great danger. An Indian on foot was poised ready to shoot him. Jeb rushed madly forward. With a quick saber thrust he wounded the Indian in the thigh. Instantly the Indian swerved around and turned his revolver upon Stuart. A shot rag out! It missed Jeb by inches. Just then Stanley and McIntyre, two other officers, came galloping up full speed to help their comrades.

"Wait! I'll fetch him!" yelled Stanley. He threw himself down from his horse so he could take a better aim. In vain, however—as he leaped down he accidentally discharged his pistol. "My last load!" he cried despairingly.

At once the Indian turned on Stanley. Slowly and deliberately the redskin moved toward him with his revolver. Jeb, drawing his saber, charged forward. Rushing at the Indian, he struck him with all his strength on the head, wounding him badly. At that same moment, with Jeb barely a foot away, the Indian shot his last load. Jeb slumped on his horse. McIntyre, rushing forward, killed the Indian.

Bleeding and weak, Jeb still managed to dismount by himself. He lay on the ground. Someone was sent for the doctor at once, but as they were now eight miles from the spot where the fighting had begun, Jeb did not see him until much later. As the bugle sounded the call to rally, numbers of the men gathered around the wounded lieutenant.

On Colonel Sumner's orders, Stuart was placed on an improvised stretcher made from a blanket and taken back to the area where the regiment would camp for the night. Bounced and jolted in his blanket stretcher for some three miles, Jeb finally met the doctor, who was coming out to examine him. He looked at Stuart's wound—luckily the Indian's bullet had glanced to the left as it entered his victim's chest—bandaged it, and accompanied him back to the camping site. As soon as he was settled, Jeb propped himself up as much as he could and settled down to a favorite occupation—writing a letter to his beloved Flora. He assured her the wound was not considered dangerous, "though I may be confined to my bed for weeks. I am now enjoying excellent health in every other respect."

Always vigorous and active, he found his forced inactivity dull and boring and spent much of his time reading the only two books available—his prayer book and his copy of Army Regulations.

It is surely a tribute to Stuart's hardy physique and magnificent stamina that only ten days after he was wounded he was able once more to ride. The frontier conditions under which he recuperated were certainly not sanitary and frontier medicine was fairly primitive. The great vigor and remarkable powers of endurance that were to characterize him during the Civil War must already have been well developed. Wounded on July 29, Stuart was on his horse ready to ride with the rest when a part of the troop left its field positions and started back toward Fort Kearney on August 8.

Their rations were gone and the group lived on fresh beef alone. With no compass in their command, they had to depend on their Pawnee guides for directions. On the morning of the fourteenth they awoke to find themselves enveloped in a pea-soup fog. To make matters worse, they also found, as Stuart wrote, "to our utter amazement and consternation that the *Pawnees are gone!*" Four endless days of fruitless roving, traveling in circles, and delay followed. Jeb, always ready to take the initiative, volunteered to lead a small party ahead and search out the way.

Guided by the stars, on the few nights when the heavens were not obscured by fog, and by his own sense of direction, he was able to bring them to Fort Kearney. They arrived—tired, wet, cold, and hungry—on August 17. They had been on the trail nine days. Eating a piece of hard bread as the beginning of his first real meal in days, Jeb declared, "This is the most delicious morsel I've ever tasted!"

A relief party sent back after Captain Foote and the men remaining in the field found them without any trouble, and within four days the sick and wounded were safely back at Fort Kearney.

Soon afterward Jeb and Flora were together once more, and it was a joyful day indeed for them when, in early September, their first child was born. This little girl her happy father insisted on calling Flora.

Indian troubles simmered down and the handsome young lieutenant was able to spend more time with his family at their quarters in Fort Riley. During this fairly leisurely period Jeb worked on two inventions. One was a device that made it easier to remove a saber from the belt and replace it quickly; and the other, called "Stuart's Lightning Horse Hitcher," made it possible to hitch or free a horse almost instantly. In October 1859, Stuart went on leave to visit friends and family in Virginia. While he was there, he rode to Washington and succeeded in having his saber invention bought and patented by the United States Government.

While he was in the capital he was asked to take a secret order to Lieutenant Colonel Robert E. Lee, who was at home at nearby Arlington. Jeb found that Lee had been ordered to command the marines being sent to Harpers Ferry to put down the uprising started there by John Brown. The instant he learned this, he urged Colonel Lee to let him go, too.

Lee, of course, knew Stuart well from the young lieutenant's cadet days at West Point and gladly took him as his aide-de-camp. During the action that followed, Stuart was sent to read a surrender demand to the leader of the insurrection, whom he was able to identify as the same "Ossawatomie" Brown he had encountered in the Kansas raids. Brown opened the door only a crack and held a carbine, cocked and ready, as he listened to Jeb. He said later, "I might have killed him, just as easy as I could kill a mosquito. . . ."

Brown refused to surrender. When Stuart heard his answer, he jumped away from the door of the arsenal where the rebels were barricaded and waved his cap in the air. At this prearranged signal, the U. S. Marines stormed the fort. The raid was successful. Brown and the other prisoners were turned over to the United States marshal, and Lee and the marines were ordered back to Washington. Stuart went with them and then, after this first brief touch with history, returned to his family in Virginia to finish his leave of absence.

Chapter III.

"JINE THE CAVALRY!"

By early 1861, everyone knew that the differences between the North and South were fast approaching a crisis. Jeb, waiting anxiously to see what would happen, requested two months' leave. Every day he seized on any source of news available. He wanted to know whether his native state of Virginia had decided to follow the lead of South Carolina in seceding from the Union. "Whatever she does, I will do!" he thought.

One day the news did come that Virginia had indeed left the Union. Almost at the same time Jeb received word of his promotion to captain, 1st U. S. Cavalry. This made no difference as far as his decision went. He sat down at once and wrote the Adjutant General, U. S. Army:

> Colonel: From a sense of duty to my native state (Va.), I hereby resign my position as an Officer in the Army of the United States.

As soon as he finished that letter he wrote another. In this one he offered his services to the Confederate Army.

The question of secession split the Cooke family as it split many others. Flora's two sisters followed the lead of their husbands—one went with the South and one the North. Her brother, John R. Cooke, joined the Confederacy. Colonel Philip St. George Cooke, her father, remained with his dragoons and soon was made a brigadier general of the United States Cavalry.

Jeb and Flora's small son had been named for his grandfather Cooke at birth but, when it became apparent that Colonel Cooke was going to stay with the Union, the baby's name was changed to James Ewell Brown, Junior.

Having written his two letters, Jeb took Flora and the children to Wytheville, Virginia. Soon after they arrived they received word that the War Department had accepted Jeb's resignation. Jeb left at once for Richmond to enlist in the Virginia Militia. There in May 1861, he was commissioned a lieutenant colonel of infantry. His first orders were to report to Colonel Thomas Jonathan Jackson at Harpers Ferry.

It is interesting to guess what Lieutenant Colonel Stuart and Colonel Jackson—who was to be named by history "Stonewall"—thought of each other in their first meeting. They were as different as day and night. Jeb was young, vigorous, full of song and laughter, loving handsome clothes and display, well fitting the title of "Cavalier" often bestowed upon him. Jackson was lean, quiet, and uncommunicative—frequently to the point of rudeness—solemn, completely careless of his appearance. Yet the two were to become fast friends. Both were very religious men—each in his own way—and both were fighters—again each in his own way. Both inspired great devotion in their men. But how different they seemed in all other ways! The swashbuckling young cavalryman was one of the few men who could tease

Jackson, and he often did, apparently to the great enjoyment of both.

When Jeb joined Colonel Jackson's unit it was in the Shenandoah Valley, where General Joseph Eggleston Johnston was trying to whip into some sort of order the Confederate units straggling in. As soon as Stuart reported, Jackson gave him the job of creating one efficiently operating cavalry troop out of the dozens of small companies assembled there. It was the custom for these little groups to elect their own officers. Discipline was usually pretty lax— or non-existent. The whole organization was very casual. Jeb had a lot of work to do.

Almost at once he got to try out his new unit. The blue troops began their invasion of Virginia and General Johnston and his army, not ready yet to give battle, fell back to Winchester. There Stuart and his little group of cavalry —only about three hundred and fifty men—guarded an area over fifty miles long and were in almost constant contact with the enemy.

This was the sort of thing Jeb loved. At almost any time he could be found out in the field leading or getting ready to lead some group, large or small, in a skirmish against the Union troops. He was almost never in camp. His men soon found that he *rewarded* them by giving them hazardous duty—that was what he liked best and he assumed everyone felt the same.

Soon Stuart received information that General Patterson was planning to throw his Union forces against General Johnston's troops at Winchester. The young lieutenant colonel sent a courier dashing off to the commanding general's headquarters with this intelligence. Johnston immediately ordered Colonel Jackson to move up and support the cavalry. Stuart and Jackson thus took the force of Patterson's attack and operated so well that only one regiment of the Virginia brigade and a single piece of artillery were required to delay Patterson effectively despite the fact that he threw a whole division against them. This engagement is known as The Affair at Falling Waters, and it enhanced the reputation of both Stuart and Jackson, as did nearly all these early encounters.

One of these occasions occurred during an operation against Patterson's army, when Stuart and a group of his men were riding along the edge of the battle area. Jeb, a handsome broad-shouldered figure sitting easily in the saddle, was alone and a little ahead of the others, completely careless—as always—of his personal safety. He came suddenly out of a thicket into an open space. He found himself face to face with about fifty Union soldiers! Only a fence across the open area separated them.

Without a moment's hesitation Jeb spurred his horse forward. "Tear down that fence!" he shouted. A command in that clear ringing voice carried weight. The surprised men complied at once. Then, while the Federals were still not sure what was happening, Jeb ordered, "Throw down your arms or you are dead men!" Bewildered, the men obeyed. They were marching meekly through the gap in the fence when Stuart's own troops came galloping up. It was discovered that he had captured—singlehanded—forty-nine men, almost an entire company of Pennsylvania Volunteers!

The abilities of Stuart and Jackson during these Falling Waters maneuvers were duly noted by their commanding officer, too. General Johnston recommended promotions for each of them. Almost at once Thomas Jonathan Jackson became a brigadier general and J. E. B. Stuart found himself a colonel.

After The Affair at Falling Waters, Jackson's troops began moving back through Winchester toward Manassas. They were to join the forces already gathered there under General P. G. T. Beauregard. This, decided Stuart, would be a good time to give a few lessons to the new recruits on how to behave at the front. The men themselves were not so enthusiastic. "The sensible thing to do," they said, "is to go to Winchester with the infantry."

When Jeb gaily led them *toward* the river—and the enemy—there were grumblings and mutterings on all sides that the young colonel must be downright crazy! The Federal line was coming straight at them—coming double-quick! Surely the colonel would let them turn back now.

They did not know Jeb. He halted his men at the edge of a grove of trees. "Dismount," he ordered. Reluctantly the men climbed down. Only a large open field separated them from the oncoming enemy. Closer and closer marched the Federals. Stuart held his men in place until the bluecoats were only two hundred yards away. Then he shouted, "Backward—march! Steady, men—keep your faces to the enemy!"

Marching backward among the trees as they moved toward their horses, the men fired their shotguns slowly as they went. The Federals were almost on top of them by the time they could remount! The perspiring men wanted to gallop away at top speed, but once again Stuart held them back. He made them move off at a slow trot.

As soon as they were out of sight of the enemy—but still not very far away—Jeb drew in his reins. A commanding figure sitting in his saddle, Stuart said, "Attention. Now I want to talk to you, men. You are brave fellows and patriotic, too, but you're ignorant of this kind of war and I'm teaching you. I want you to observe that a good man and a good horse can never be caught. Another thing: cavalry can trot away from anything, and a gallop is a gait unbecoming to a soldier, unless he is going *toward* the enemy. Remember that. We gallop toward the enemy, and trot away, always. Steady now. Don't break ranks."

As he said this an ominous whine started. It grew louder and louder. Suddenly a shell whistled over their heads. Stuart sat absolutely calm. "There," he announced matter-of-factly. "I've been waiting for that, and watching those fellows. I knew they'd shoot too high, and I wanted you to learn how shells sound."

For two or three days Stuart kept this little group with him inside the Federal lines. Dozens of times they were charged at, surrounded, shelled. Dozens of times they engaged in small skirmishes with the enemy. By the time their "schooling" was over, they had begun to feel a sort of amazed hero-worship for their dashing young colonel who hourly proved himself a genius when it came to getting into and out of dangerous situations. "I'd follow him anywhere," they vowed to each other.

Stuart was often accused of being reckless, but no one could ever say that he sent any of his men where he himself was not ready to go. He was always in the front or among his men, fighting. One of his soldiers said, "He could never be still. He was rarely in camp, and he never showed fatigue. He led almost everything."

On July 16 the resplendent new Union Army began its march toward Manassas. New tents, new and improved weapons, fine new uniforms—they had the best of everything money could buy. And they were on their way to meet what seemed a motley crew. The conglomerate Confederate organization was armed mostly with old smoothbore muskets in the infantry and shotguns and sabers in the cavalry. One cavalry company did not even have those—it was armed only with the pikes seized from John Brown at Harpers Ferry. The whole Southern aggregation numbered only about 20,000, in opposition to a Federal force of some 35,000.

The movement of the Federal Army had a holiday air. United States congressmen and their families packed picnic lunches and rode from nearby Washington to see the battle. They were completely confident that the Union Army would easily overwhelm the Southern forces and move triumphantly on to Richmond. The war would be over before it had even begun!

And things did look dark for the Southern troops at Manassas. A group of Federals tried to force their way across the stream of Bull Run and, though they were driven back, General Beauregard knew they would renew their attack the next day and no doubt come across in force. He sent a message to General Johnston at Winchester: "If you're going to help me, now is the time!"

Johnston, getting ready to move to Beauregard's aid, sent Stuart out to screen his movements from the enemy. The young colonel and his cavalrymen chased in pickets, harassed outposts with enthusiasm, and in general acted with such audacity and vigor that Union General Patterson, far from thinking the main body of troops had withdrawn, was convinced that Johnston's whole army—"at least 35,000 men," he estimated—was about to attack *him!* He did not even discover Johnston was gone until July 21, the actual day of the Battle of Manassas.

Though their job of screening the infantry's movements made it necessary for them to get off to a late start, Stuart's cavalry reached Manassas in time to play an important part in the battle. They had covered sixty miles in two days.

Stuart's job in this battle was to cover Jackson's left flank, and it was from that position that the cavalry turned back assault after assault. At one point in the fighting a heavy drift of artillery smoke covered the hill where Jackson's troops were. As it faded away, Stuart rode out from among a group of trees. He saw a regiment, scarlet uniforms bright in the summer sunshine, running toward him. There was a red-clad Alabama unit in the field that day and Stuart thought this was it. Seeing them running toward him and thinking they were in retreat, Jeb, with about three hundred of his men, rode out to meet them. "Don't run, boys," he called in his clear ringing voice. "We are here."

Just then a gust of wind blew out their flag—Federals! Dark plume waving on his hat, Stuart spurred his horse forward and led his men straight into the enemy ranks. Federal shots rang out. Nine Confederate soldiers and eighteen horses were killed, but the force of Stuart's drive scattered the Yankees, and that group could not be gathered again. More enemy infantry came charging forward and Stuart and his men had to return to the woods on Jackson's left. There more Union attempts to turn the infantry's flank were pushed back.

It was during this fighting that General Jackson, making a splendid stand with his brigade just when it seemed the Confederates were about to be overwhelmed, earned his famous nickname. General Bee saw him and shouted in admiration, "There is Jackson standing like a stone wall!"

Finally the last Confederate reserve, Colonel Jubal Early's brigade, moved forward, Confederate guns opened up along the turnpike, and the Federal troops began their retreat. This retreat soon disintegrated into a rout. Little groups of Confederate cavalry galloped about gathering up prisoners as long as there was enough daylight to see by.

Newly promoted Brigadier General Jubal Early (his new rank bore the date of the Battle of Bull Run) said later, "But for his [Stuart's] presence there, I am of the opinion that my brigade would have arrived too late to be of any service. . . .

"Stuart did as much towards saving the battle of First Manassas as any subordinate who participated in it. . . ."

General Johnston, too, appreciated Stuart's contribution in this battle. He wrote Jefferson Davis, President of the Confederacy, a letter recommending Stuart's promotion and said:

"He is a rare man, wonderfully endowed by nature with the qualities necessary for an officer of light cavalry. Calm, firm, acute, active, and enterprising, I know no one more competent than he to estimate the occurrences before him at their true value. If you add a real brigade of cavalry to this army, you cannot find a better brigadier-general to command it."

President Davis evidently agreed, for on September 24, 1861, he sent forward a commission making James Ewell Brown Stuart a brigadier general of cavalry in the Provisional Army of the Confederate States of America.

After the First Battle of Manassas, or Bull Run, there was a period of comparative quiet. The main armies were inactive several months but even during this time the new brigadier general of cavalry was busy. His troops were frequently engaged in small skirmishing actions and were often out on reconnaissance. Once again Stuart used a lull in the fighting as a period of instruction for green troops and he himself acted as their teacher. One of these little expeditions Jeb particularly enjoyed.

A former West Point classmate of Stuart's, Orlando M. Poe, was now a Union cavalry officer. He was stationed not too far from Stuart's outposts. The little crossroads village where Poe and his men were often found itself the goal of small reconnaissance parties of Confederates. One day Poe sent Stuart a message:

> Dear Beauty—come and see me sometime. I invite you to dine with me at Willard's Hotel in Washington next Saturday night. Meantime, keep the Black Horse off me, will you?

Jeb received the invitation on a Wednesday. His reply was quick—and typical. The very next day he rode into Poe's camp and took it completely by surprise. Blue-coated troopers leaped on their horses and raced off in all directions!

When Stuart sent in his report of the action he enclosed Poe's invitation to him and wrote on the back:

"From the manner in which Captain Poe left here, he was going in to get that dinner without waiting for Saturday night!" Jeb thought the whole affair was a wonderful joke and enjoyed it immensely.

This period of skirmishing and frequent brushes with the enemy made the abilities of certain of the men and officers in the cavalry troop stand out, and Stuart noted them well as he began selecting his staff. Young John Pelham from Alabama—tall, blond, and handsome enough to create a furor in feminine hearts wherever he went—came to the fore as he started to show the abilities that were to give him an immortal name as a master of artillery. Laughing Fitz Lee, nephew of General Robert E. Lee and former West Point schoolmate of Jeb's, had begun to demonstrate his outstanding military talents too. Stuart was to count on them in many emergencies.

Mrs. Stuart and the two children were frequent visitors to Jeb's headquarters at the camp he had named Qui Vive. In these early months of the war before battles became frequent, Mrs. Stuart was often able to be with her husband or to stay not far from where he was stationed. Stuart, a devoted husband and father, was never happier than when he could be with his family. When his military duties kept them apart, Jeb wrote Flora almost every day, often scribbling a note to her from horseback as he rode on some military mission.

The Stuart who appeared in camp and the Stuart who appeared on the battlefield were quite different. Off duty, Jeb was gay, boisterous, and seemed boyish and carefree. He gloried in elegant and beautiful clothes, enjoyed balls and singing. He and his column, accompanied by the banjo player Sweeney, whom Stuart kept with him whenever possible, would break into Stuart's favorite "Jine the Cavalry" at the drop of a hat, making the woods or camp resound with their singing. It is said that General Longstreet once laughingly ordered Jeb from his camp, saying, "You make life in the cavalry seem so attractive that all my infantrymen will be wanting to desert and 'jine the cavalry.'"

On the battlefield the young and carefree boy changed into a calm, farsighted, and skilled commander, a fearless and courageous leader whose deeds inspired his troops. In victory or defeat—though he never could really bring himself to admit defeat—he remained cheerful and alert. Even his critics admit his tremendous military skill and say that his main deficiencies grew out of the fact that he was brave even to the point of foolhardiness. Federal troops feared no Southern leader more and the Northern cavalry leaders—Buford, Sheridan, and Pleasonton—against whom he so often matched wits, had the greatest respect for his abilities.

Jeb's fame had now grown to the point where he received presents from people he had never seen. A lady of Maryland sent him a fine spyglass he carried the rest of the war; someone else sent him golden spurs for his boots. Another gift, and one that Jeb especially appreciated, was that of a splendid horse called the Star of the East. Jeb exclaimed with pleasure, "I'm now better mounted than any general in the army!"

Stuart always had an eye for the beautiful horses he loved. A young cavalryman, assigned to some work at the headquarters of Camp Qui Vive, had finished his task one day and was waiting on the porch for further orders. Stuart came out. Immediately he noticed the young man's mount, which stood nearby.

"Is that your horse?" he asked. He walked up to the animal and started looking it over intently.

"Yes, sir," was the reply.

Stuart continued his examination. Then, while he stood patting the horse's nose, he asked the young man if he would like to sell him. The owner assured him he would not. The young general continued to look over the mount. Then he turned suddenly to the young cavalryman and said, "Let's slip off on a scout, then; I'll ride your horse and you can ride mine. I want to try your beast's paces."

In a second the two had leaped on the horses and were galloping away. Stuart led the way to the Confederate outpost. Past the gray picket they went, a last sentinel on the road leading toward the enemy lines. On they rode.

Stuart headed off through the fields. He wanted to see how the borrowed horse would do on rough ground. His companion said later, "Where or how far he intended to go I did not know. He was enamored of my horse, and rode,

I suppose, for the pleasure of riding an animal which pleased him."

They raced on until some blue-coated cavalry noticed them and began to pursue. Jeb, cloak flying in the breeze, cut onto another road that led through the woods and back to the Confederate camp. The young cavalryman was worried. He knew this area well. "General," he called, "there is a Federal picket post just ahead of us. Hadn't we better oblique into the woods?"

"Oh no," replied Stuart nonchalantly. "They won't expect us from this direction." This was likely—the two Confederates would be coming from *behind* them! "We can ride over them before they make up their minds who we are," he continued.

Stuart dug in his spurs—the horses leaped forward. Racing ahead at full speed, the two riders went tearing past the astonished bluecoats. They were a full hundred yards beyond the picket line before the amazed soldiers could even fire. The musket balls zoomed by.

There was no more conversation until the two riders were back at Camp Qui Vive. Then Jeb said casually, "Did you ever time this horse for a half mile?"

The largest engagement of this period was the Battle of Dranesville. On December 20, Stuart, with four regiments of infantry, a battery of artillery, and 150 cavalry, was ordered to cover a foraging wagon train sent out to collect supplies from the farms west of the town. By chance that same morning some 4000 Union troops, with two additional infantry brigades in support, also moved into Dranesville. The Confederate pickets were chased away from the area, but for some reason sent no message back to their lines.

Completely unaware of what they were going into,

Stuart and his troops moved serenely on toward the town. At the same time the wagons moved off to the west to forage. When the Confederates approached Dranesville they discovered the enemy—already there and drawn up in battle formation! Federal soldiers had even started out in search of the wagon trains. There was only one course of action. Though outnumbered, Stuart had to attack to give his foragers time to move out of danger. He advanced at once.

Federal artillery was already firmly entrenched on the higher ground and so commanded the area. Confederate guns were never able to fire effectively from the exposed position they were forced to assume. Neither could the gray artillery protect itself from the enemy's fire, and it suffered heavy casualties. The green Confederate troops fired at each other too—a mistake that seems to have been made by most green troops in most wars.

For two hours Stuart and his men fought stubbornly against the entrenched Federals, although they were able to inflict little real damage. Then, having accomplished their purpose of engaging the enemy until the wagon trains could be moved back to a safe position, they withdrew. It turned out that they left just at the right time, too, for even as they were moving out, two additional Union brigades were coming up to join the fight. The next day the gray troopers, reinforced by additional cavalry and infantry, moved against Dranesville again, only to find that the enemy had retired from the area during the night.

In this engagement Stuart lost 194 men, the enemy only 68. Despite this defeat, the men felt even more confidence in their young general because of the skill he had shown in getting them out of their extremely dangerous position.

Chapter IV.

ONCE AROUND McCLELLAN

In the spring of 1862 the large, well-equipped Union Army started slowly moving southward under its new commanding officer—hailed as "the young Napoleon of the West"—General George B. McClellan. After the engagements that followed—Yorktown, Williamsburg, Seven Pines —the cavalry acted as a screen for the Confederate Army in its movements.

Often the battles of the main armies took place on marshy terrain that made the use of cavalry impossible, but even then Stuart himself did not sit idly by. He refused to be a spectator. The dashing figure in the plumed hat could often be seen moving about where the shells were flying thickest. He was busy in several engagements, acting as General Longstreet's means of communication with the battlefield. In his official report after the Battle of Seven Pines, Longstreet said, "Brigadier General J. E. B. Stuart, in the absence of any opportunity to use his cavalry, was of material service by his presence with me on the field."

It was in this battle that General J. E. Johnston was severely wounded. He was replaced by General Robert E. Lee, who was put in command of the Army of Northern Virginia.

Lee looked over the situation to plan his future strategy. McClellan's well-equipped army of about 115,000 men had moved into entrenched positions along the marshy bed of the Chickahominy River. Their supply and communications lines stretched back all the way to the White House on the Pamunkey (an old family home of the Lees, it so happened) near the York River. Perhaps, thought Lee, Jackson's corps could move secretly down the Valley of Virginia and fall suddenly on the right wing of McClellan's army while Lee attacked from the front. If the maneuver were successful, the whole Union Army might be destroyed!

If such a move were to be attempted, Lee would need exact and accurate information as to the position of McClellan's right flank. To get this information Lee called in Stuart. They had a conference on June 10, and the next day Lee issued a written order authorizing a cavalry scouting expedition. In it he said, "You are desired to make a scout movement to the rear of the enemy now posted on the Chickahominy, with a view of gaining intelligence of his operations, communications, etc., and of driving in his foraging parties and securing such grain, cattle, etc., for ourselves as you can make arrangements to have driven in. Another object is to destroy his wagon trains. . . ." And then, having known the sometimes reckless young Jeb since his West Point cadet days, Lee went on to caution him, "You will return as soon as the object of your expedition is accomplished, and you must bear constantly in mind, while endeavoring to execute the general purpose of your mission, not to hazard unnecessarily your command. . . ."

The commanding general then gave particulars on the organization of the raiding party. He was never to bother to again. After this, their first large operation together, he had such confidence in Jeb that his later instructions to him were very loose and general. Indeed, many people have thought they were too much so.

Jeb quietly and carefully went about choosing the best 1200 troopers in his command. His eyes gleamed with excitement, but he didn't indicate in any way what was afoot. The men themselves must have hazarded a few guesses as to where they were going when they were told to pack three days' rations in their haversacks.

Even Jeb's staff could only speculate. General Lee had said secrecy must be observed and Stuart intended to see that it was. To command the three cavalry units Jeb chose Colonel W. T. Martin and the two Lees. Both Lees were colonels and they were also first cousins—Fitz, Robert E. Lee's nephew, and William H. F. ("Rooney"), General Lee's second oldest son, a quiet, handsome, and capable young man of twenty-five. Young Lieutenant James Breathed was in charge of the two light guns of the Stuart horse artillery.

Also included in the expedition was Heros Von Borcke. This huge Prussian from the 3rd Dragoon Guards of the Royal Prussian Army had run the Northern blockade to join the Confederacy. When he made his application to join Stuart's command not long before the Battle of Seven Pines, he had appeared in full hunting regalia—pink coat, white breeches, top boots, and an enormous dragoon sword! Stuart, of course, could not resist such flamboyance and accepted him on the spot. At Seven Pines they had ridden together and the Prussian's courage and efficiency under fire made Jeb feel he would be valuable on this expedition.

Three of the most famous scouts in the Confederate Army were chosen, too. They were Redmond Burke, the renowned William Downes Farley, and John Mosby, "the Grey Ghost of the Confederacy," later one of the best-known guerrilla fighters of the war.

At two o'clock on the morning of June 12, Stuart himself —already up and ready to go—roused his officers. "Gentlemen," he said, "in ten minutes every man must be in the saddle." At once the camp was astir. The men moved quickly and quietly. Soon the long column, unheralded by flag or bugle, was on its way, it knew not where nor why. Thus began the famous Chickahominy Raid.

John Esten Cooke, one of Stuart's staff, wrote of Jeb's appearance as he started on one of his most famous exploits:

"As he mounted his horse on that moonlight night he was a gallant figure to look at. The gray coat buttoned to the chin, the light French sabre, the pistol in its black holster; the cavalry boots above the knee, and the brown hat with its black plume floating above the bearded features, the brilliant eyes and the huge mustache, which curled with laughter at the slightest provocation—these made Stuart the perfect picture of a gay cavalier, and the spirited horse he rode seemed to feel that he carried one whose motto was to 'do or die.'"

In order to hide his real purpose as long as possible, Stuart marched his column straight north for twenty-two miles. Everyone assumed the column was going to join Jackson's troops in the valley. As they rode through the infantry camps along Brook Turnpike, the infantrymen shouted to them, "Why are you riding up to join Old Stonewall? Why don't you stay here where the fighting is?"

An old army friend of Stuart's passed them on the way and said, "How long you going to be gone, Beauty?"

Jeb turned in his saddle and laughed as he called after him, singing the words of a popular song of the day,

> "Oh, it may be for years
> And it may be forever."

The next day the newspapers mentioned that Lee was sending reinforcements to Jackson in the valley.

It was beginning to be obvious to Jeb's troops, however, that their young general had something quite different in mind. That first night they camped without campfires. Nor were there the usual brassy notes of Reveille to tumble them from their bedrolls the next morning. In silence they were roused and had their breakfast. Then, still early in the gray dawn of June 13, they quietly swung into their saddles—no bugle proclaimed "Boots and Saddles!"—and followed Stuart as he turned abruptly away from their northward route and struck out almost directly to the east.

Till this moment Jeb alone had known the true purpose of their mission. Now he took his three colonels into his confidence "so as to secure an intelligent action and co-operation in whatever might occur," as he said. Their first goal was to reach the Old Church area. This lay directly behind the rear of McClellan's right wing commander, General Fitz-John Porter.

To get there they had to pass through the village of Hanover Court House. Federal troops had been reported in that area, so Jeb sent Fitz Lee and his 1st Virginia Regiment to move around to the enemy's rear. Meanwhile Stuart was to attack them from the front. When the time to attack came, the main Confederate column went charging forward, sabers drawn and ready. Clouds of dust and smoke rose as the two forces met. The Federals soon retreated. Unfortunately no Fitz Lee was waiting to cut them off—he had been delayed in reaching the assigned position—and they hurried off southward.

Fitz Lee soon rejoined the main column and they moved on toward Old Church. At first they met no one, but their movements had been reported and a group of about a hundred Union cavalry under Captain Royall were already galloping up Old Church Road to meet them. When they first clashed in a brief skirmish at Totopotomoy Creek, the leading Federal horsemen were ridden over and jammed back against the main body of troops. In the pursuit that followed Stuart noted with pleasure Lieutenant W. T. Robins, who did just the sort of thing Jeb himself loved to do: "On, on dashed Robins, here skirting a field, there leaping a fence or ditch, and clearing the woods beyond, when not far from Old Church, the enemy made a stand, having been reenforced."

Captain Royall rallied his forces and drew them up to meet the expected Confederate attack. Stuart shouted, "Form fours! Draw sabers! Charge!" A squadron of the 9th Virginia Regiment sprang forward.

Their handsome young leader, Captain Latané, yelled, "On to them, boys!" Half rising in his stirrups and with sword in hand, he spurred his horse forward, leading the charge. Instantly he and Captain Royall were locked in hand-to-hand combat. A moment later both had fallen—Royall badly wounded from Latané's saber thrust and

Latané, never to rise again, having been shot and killed instantly.

The Federals broke in confusion, fled, rallied, and, hit this time by a squadron of Colonel "Rooney" Lee's men, fled again. Fitz Lee's regiment galloped quickly to the front to lead the pursuit. They followed the bluecoats to their camp—deserted now by the fleeing soldiers—and destroyed it.

Many Union soldiers were captured, but many others escaped through the woods. One of them, an officer, reported to headquarters his amazing impression that three to five regiments of infantry were supporting the Confederate cavalry!

By the middle of the afternoon General Porter's cavalry commander—who was none other than Jeb's father-in-law, Brigadier General Philip St. George Cooke—had received numerous reports of Stuart's operations. He had also received the report of the mythical three to five infantry regiments. Therefore he requested infantry and artillery to reinforce his own cavalry. The delay this caused the Federals, as well as a wait for forage—they'd discovered they had none after they'd started out—gave the Confederates valuable time.

Jeb said later, "Here was the turning point of the expedition." He had the information Lee had wanted: he knew that the Federal right wing had not been extended toward Hanover Court House and the railroad—it was, in military parlance, "in the air." The question now was—what was the best way to get this information back to the commanding general?

Jeb had a vital decision to make. There were two routes open to him—he could go back the same way he had come, or he could ride completely around the Federal Army and cross the Chickahominy at one of the lower fords. He stroked his red-gold beard reflectively as he weighed the possible courses of action.

Stuart knew that the presence of Federal cavalry at Hanover Court House that morning indicated a much larger body somewhere nearby. By the time he could get back that evening they would be gathered there in force. On the other hand, if he went forward instead of backward, he would have a much longer route. He would have to take the outside line of march, moving along a road very close to enemy camps in some places. The Federals could move rapidly along the shorter inside lines. They had the use of several roads giving easy access to the route Stuart would probably travel, too.

The fact that several good local guides were in the expeditionary force may have influenced Stuart. One of these, Lieutenant Jones Christian, whose home was a farm on the Chickahominy, had offered to guide them to the ford on his property.

Jeb turned in his saddle and said to Esten Cooke, who was riding beside him, "Tell Fitz Lee to come along. I'm going to move on with my column." Without any apparent hesitation Stuart led his men forward. If he were worried about the gravity of the decision he was making, nobody with him could tell. In fact almost no one even seemed to suspect that the decisive moment of the expedition had come—and gone.

When Stuart told his fellow officers of his decision, he reported that "While none accorded a full assent, all assured me a hearty support in whatever I did." So, with what Jeb called "an abiding trust in God, and with such guarantees of success as the two Lees and Martin and their devoted followers," the column turned eastward. The die was cast.

The reaction of his troops, moving into what certainly appeared the most dangerous situation they had ever been in, pleased and delighted Jeb. He said exultantly, "There was something sublime in the implicit confidence and unquestioning trust of the rank and file in a leader guiding them straight, apparently, into the very jaws of the enemy, every step appearing to them to diminish the faintest hope of extrication."

The staff officers, too, thought the chances of the column's getting through were pretty slim. John Esten Cooke estimated they had about one chance in ten of getting out alive. He said, after it was obvious Stuart planned to ride *around* McClellan, "It was neck or nothing, now."

Perhaps the course of action Jeb had chosen would have seemed less fearsome to his men had they known what the alternate route offered. By this time three Federal cavalry regiments and an entire brigade of infantry had gathered on the road to Hanover Court House. Hence a return by that route would appear to have been quite effectively closed off.

If this large group had taken off at once in pursuit of the Confederates they could no doubt have added greatly to the hazards of Stuart's safe return. But the Federals were not sure how large the raiding column was (they were still concerned about those three to five regiments of infantry), and General Porter ordered Brigadier General Cooke to advance with great caution. All of this gave Stuart the time he needed.

Now Jeb was able to carry out the second part of Lee's

instructions—to destroy any enemy supplies he came across. Their route lay across McClellan's main supply lines and they had many opportunities to take advantage of this. Supply wagons moving unconcernedly along the road, unaware that any Confederates were within miles, were captured in numbers. Stuart sent two squadrons of men to Putney's Ferry. There they burned two large supply-laden transports and destroyed wagons from a supply train.

As they rode, suddenly they heard a shout: "Yankees to the rear!" The whole column wheeled around instantly! Nothing was behind them. There was a burst of laughter and soon the whole column joined in. They enjoyed the joke all afternoon.

Jeb sent a small group of hand-picked men to make the railroad impassable. Farley, Burke, Mosby, and Von Borcke led the way. Without firing a shot they captured the fifteen infantrymen guarding the depot. Scout Redmond Burke set fire to a nearby bridge. Some of the others went to work chopping down telegraph poles.

Suddenly the long whistle of an approaching train could be heard above all the noise and confusion. Hurriedly the men rushed to block the track, but time was against them. The train roared into view. The gray troopers hustled into hiding. Perhaps they could ambush the train if it stopped. The engine ground to a near halt. A passenger or two alighted. Suddenly a shot rang out. One of the concealed Confederate cavalrymen could not control his excitement —he had fired too soon.

Instantly the engineer yelled, "Full steam ahead!" The train shot forward. Gray troopers galloped beside the train, shooting as they went. The Federal soldiers huddled on the open flatcars returned their fire.

Captain Farley and Von Borcke galloped beside the train, too. Scout Farley grabbed Von Borcke's blunderbuss and urged his horse forward at full speed. He overtook the engine and fired into the cab, hitting the engineer. On sped the train, out of range almost at once.

Now they were only four miles from McClellan's main supply base, the White House on the Pamunkey, which had been in happier days "Rooney" Lee's plantation home. Stuart was greatly tempted by the thought of all the Federal supplies that could be destroyed there, but the risk was too great. Though he admitted he "could scarcely resist it," he wisely decided not to attack in that direction.

Instead he contented himself with destroying the property available at Tunstall's Station. There was a good bit to be contented with, however—a loaded wagon train, railroad cars loaded and standing at the depot ready to leave, other rolling stock, and a railroad bridge were all destroyed. A sutler's stores of delicacies for sale to Union soldiers and rations from the captured supply wagons were handed out to the hungry Confederate troopers. What a feast they had on this Yankee abundance!

As dark came on their position grew more and more dangerous. Stuart assembled his men—still eating as they mounted their horses—and led them on toward Talleysville, seven miles away. "Rooney" Lee, so close to home, must have felt deeply as he rode past long-familiar landmarks in the deepening twilight.

Meanwhile at his erstwhile home, the White House on the Pamunkey, there was much agitation. Everyone was sure the dashing dark-plumed Confederate cavalryman would be leading his troops down upon them any minute! Federals ran hither and thither. Every man who could carry a gun—be he clerk, teamster, sick or wounded—was given a weapon and sent out to strengthen the regular guard. McClellan's quartermaster was working feverishly to protect his supplies.

Jeb and his men rode on (the quartermaster's fears came to nought). Trotting along in the moonlight, the men, exhausted, swayed and fell asleep in their saddles. The column reached Talleysville about 9 P.M. and there their hardy young general finally let them halt. The weary troopers fairly fell to the ground. They were asleep instantly.

The Confederate cavalrymen had covered some thirty five miles since morning. It had been a day full of hard riding and hard fighting. The sleepy soldiers thought the three hours of rest they were allowed were gone almost before they had closed their eyes.

When the brief rest was over, some of the men exchanged their tired horses for fresher mounts from among the animals captured earlier. Prisoners were sorted out, organized, and given horses. Pockets and saddlebags bulged as the gray troopers tried to stuff all the captured supplies possible into them.

The gaiety of the men during this midnight break was surprising. They laughed, they sang, they joked as they gorged themselves on the Yankee supplies. (Esten Cooke reported eating "in succession" figs, beef tongue, pickle, candy, tomato catsup, preserves, lemons, cakes, sausages, molasses, crackers, and canned meats!)

They realized now that they were riding completely *around* McClellan's army! The daring and boldness of this maneuver filled them with excitement and fired their imaginations. They felt capable of any deeds of derring-do!

Their vigorous young general shared their feelings. His

laugh rang out and his blue eyes sparkled—this was the good time they had all hoped to have when they "jined the cavalry!" When "Boots and Saddles!" sounded, every man leaped eagerly upon his horse. They were ready for anything! Let Jeb Stuart lead them where he would! With his eager men following, the general headed straight southward. Pointing out the way was Lieutenant Jones Christian, toward whose home and private ford they were heading.

The gray column got off not a moment too soon. Only two hours later the first of the Federals, Rush's Lancers, galloped up to the very area where Jeb and his men had spent the night. Already bone-tired, the Federals stopped and rested four hours.

It was a good thing for the Confederates that Rush did not know he was only four hours behind them. Stuart and his men were finding the going slow and heavy. Recent rains had made the roads muddy and the artillery particularly was making little progress. The rigors of the expedition were beginning to tell on them all. Cooke said, "Whole companies went to sleep in the saddle, and Stuart himself was no exception. He had thrown one knee over the pommel of his saddle, folded his arms, dropped the bridle, and —chin on breast, his plumed hat drooping over his forehead —was sound asleep." So they moved on through the darkness, sleepwalking, so to speak, toward their last real barrier to safety, the Chickahominy.

Ahead of them this river was undergoing a transformation. The usually quiet little brackish stream, easily fordable in dozens of places, had been changed by the heavy spring rains into a swift and dangerous river. Its fast waters swirled out rapidly into the surrounding swamplands. When the Confederate advance guard reached the river about daylight, Christian's Ford had completely disappeared.

Colonel "Rooney" Lee volunteered to try to swim his horse across the swollen stream. Stripping off most of his clothes, the tall, handsome young man guided his horse into the dark water. A few of his men followed. It proved a touch-and-go affair in the treacherous current. Though they made it, everyone saw it was too hazardous for the whole group to try. Lee refused to leave his command and so, with his men watching anxiously from the muddy bank, he made the dangerous swim back to rejoin them.

When he returned to the rest of the column and climbed ashore on his dripping horse, someone asked, "What do you think of the situation, Colonel?"

"Well," Lee said, "I think we are caught."

Next they tried felling trees along the riverbank with the idea of building a temporary log bridge. This did not work either. The rushing Chickahominy had seized the logs as though they were mere twigs and had swept them downstream in its swirling waters just as the main body of troops arrived. Every eye in the command turned to Jeb Stuart. What in the world could they do now? Sitting calmly on his charger, Stuart quietly stroked his bright beard, a gesture he often used when deep in thought. He dispatched a courier to General Robert E. Lee telling him their situation. In the message he requested that the infantry create some sort of diversion in front of the left wing of McClellan's army, behind which the cavalry had yet to pass.

No sooner had he sent this message than a report came that the remains of an old bridge lay a few miles down the river. Instantly Jeb swung into action. Christian's Ford was abandoned. The column dug in their spurs and galloped quickly to the old bridge.

The bridge had been partly burned, but the pilings were

still standing. Nearby was an old warehouse. Stuart at once ordered everyone to work tearing it down. Even the prisoners offered enthusiastic assistance!

While the work went on, Mosby looked at Jeb, who was casually "lying down on the bank of the stream, in the gayest humor I ever saw, laughing at the prank he had played on McClellan." Later Stuart—general or not—was working, too, putting planks down and singing while he worked. In a miraculously short time the bridge was laid.

As soon as the bridge frame was finished the cavalrymen started across, holding the bridles of their horses, which swam alongside. Half the group crossed this way while the bridge was being strengthened and enlarged. After only three hours of work it could bear the weight of the artillery and the rest of the cavalry mounted. By 1 P.M. the whole expedition had crossed.

Fitz Lee was the last man over. While the bridge building was going on, his rear guard had driven off several small groups of Federal cavalry. As he trotted up the southern bank, the first of Rush's Lancers came galloping madly out of the woods opposite and started to shoot at him. Immediately Lee's men set fire to the bridge. They and their young colonel quickly galloped off to join the rest of the column.

Farther on they had to ford what was usually a quiet, tractable little branch of the Chickahominy, now risen to new height and rapidity. It was here they suffered their only loss of equipment—a limber from one of the cannons.

The worst was over. Nevertheless they were still at least twenty miles within enemy lines. This twenty-mile ride would have to be along the James River, filled with Union gunboats on one side and General Hooker's blue infantry on the other. These seemed small dangers, however, in comparison to the ones through which they had just passed. Jeb —and his whole column with him—were filled with a sense of carefree gaiety.

It was now late afternoon of June 14; they had been on the road almost three days. Moving forward without rest, the column at last reached Buckland, where they bivouacked at the home of Colonel J. M. Wilcox. For the first time in thirty-six hours the men were able to tumble from their saddles. They threw themselves on the ground thankfully and were asleep in seconds.

Jeb himself did not stop. Leaving orders with Fitz Lee to rouse the men and move on at eleven that night, he took a courier and Frayser, a guide whose work had been very valuable on this expedition, and galloped on. He knew every minute was precious to General Lee, so he rode through the night to make his report. He reached Richmond just before dawn on June 15.

Jeb sent Frayser to tell Flora of his safe return. He himself went straight to General Lee's headquarters. There he was able to report that the expedition had captured 165 prisoners and 260 animals, had destroyed a quantity of valuable Federal property, and, most important of all, had gained information that was to prove of great value. In fact many people credit this information with making possible the movements which resulted in the Confederate victory at Cold Harbor twelve days later. Stuart's daring expedition had been accomplished with only one battle casualty, Captain Latané.

After Stuart had made his report he rode back to rejoin his column and lead it into camp. This was a triumphant affair. The word of the expedition's exploit had traveled like wildfire. Crowds gathered, ladies waved dainty handkerchiefs, spontaneous cheers rang out. Stuart gloried in it all. His amazing physical endurance—he had been some forty-eight hours in the saddle without sleep—enabled him to look as fresh and vigorous as ever.

The unshaven, dirty, tired soldiers astride their weary horses enjoyed the procession too. They grinned at the crowd's reception and when the golden voice at the head of the column rang out in song, they joined in:

> *"If you want to smell hell—*
> *If you want to have fun—*
> *If you want to catch the devil—*
> *Jine the Cavalry!"*

Not only was the local audience at the homecoming excited. The expedition made a tremendous impression on everyone. Jeb's name was on every tongue. Southern newspapers were jubilant. Even some of the Northern ones admitted their admiration. Many people felt the success of the raid shook the confidence of the North in McClellan's abilities. Surely the expedition gave a tremendous boost to the morale, not only of the Confederate cavalry, but of the whole Confederate Army.

After the whole operation was over, one of Stuart's friends, talking about the column's plight when they found the Chickahominy was no longer fordable, said, "That was a tight place at the river, General. If the enemy had come down on us, you would have been compelled to have surrendered."

"No," replied Jeb, "one other course was left."

"What was that?" his companion asked.

"To die game."

Chapter V.

GUNBOATS
AND LEMONADE

Using the information Stuart had gained on his Chickahominy Raid, Lee began to make his plans for attack. Jackson was to come down secretly from the Shenandoah
Valley. He would march along the north side of the Chickahominy and fall upon the right flank of McClellan's army.
Other Confederate divisions under A. P. Hill, D. H. Hill,
and Longstreet would attack at the same time. This strategy
required close coordination of all the different units if it
were to succeed—and lack of this was to prove its weakness.

Jeb's part in the plan was to move with Jackson's troops,
protecting their front and flanks and guiding them to Mc-
Clellan's right flank, which he had reconnoitered on his
recent raid. Stuart and his column were at their appointed
place at the appointed time, but Jackson, who seemed dis-
interested and lethargic throughout this campaign, was some
nine hours late. Some of the other Confederate commanders
got tired of waiting for Jackson and went ahead and attacked without him. There is no record of what Stuart

thought, but he must certainly have been surprised—and impatient to get into action—when Jackson calmly had his men make camp within hearing of the sounds of battle.

In the series of engagements that followed—known collectively as the Seven Days' Battle—the terrain was often too swampy to make use of the cavalry. Stuart himself was always in the thick of things, however. He was frequently accompanied by the author John Esten Cooke, Flora's cousin. Cooke wrote that they were often amidst "shelling hotter than I ever knew it. . . . I followed Stuart here, there, *everywhere.*"

In one of these engagements in which the cavalry could not operate because of the terrain, Stuart sent forward two of his guns under the command of Captain John Pelham. The skill and bravery of this young artillery officer from Alabama were to make the adjective "gallant" almost a part of his name. With only one artillery piece Pelham carried on an unequal attack upon two entire Federal batteries. Jeb reported proudly that, though the enemy fire directed upon the little group of Confederate artillerymen was fearsome, "yet not a man quailed, and the noble captain [directed] the fire himself with a coolness and intrepidity only equalled by his previous brilliant career." Pelham's work had its effect; Stuart noted that "The enemy's fire sensibly slackened under the determined fire of this Napoleon [the type of artillery piece the Confederates used]."

Later in the Seven Days' Battle, when the Federal lines at Gaines' Mill and Cold Harbor had been breached, Stuart and his men went forward in pursuit. From there they moved on toward the White House on the Pamunkey. This was familiar territory, the same through which they had passed on the Chickahominy Raid.

Encountering some opposition near Old Cold Harbor, they soon sent it on its way. Then the cavalrymen busied themselves cutting telegraph wires and tearing up railroad tracks. At Tunstall's Station Stuart called up Pelham and his guns to take care of the squadron of Federal cavalry entrenched on the opposite bank of Black Creek. Pelham's fire sent the blue cavalry scurrying and, as an extra dividend, flushed out an unsuspected Federal ambush which had been lying in wait for any Confederates who might try to cross the stream.

That night they bivouacked at Tunstall's Station. They could see great clouds of smoke darkening the skies and hear frequent explosions. The Federals were destroying their supplies in the Union quartermaster depot at nearby White House. Stuart wrote that the huge fire "raged fearfully during the entire night."

On the next day, June 29, Stuart led his troops toward the White House. They advanced very cautiously, as the local citizens had told Jeb that there were at least 5000 Federals—a force far outnumbering the Confederates—on guard at the supply base.

As they approached the camp it became evident that the Union soldiers had already moved out. The only present evidence of Federal occupation was the gunboat *Marblehead*, which still held a commanding position in the river. At this stage of the war even the word "gunboat" struck terror into the hearts of most of the soldiers. Strong men quailed at the thought of its huge shells shrieking nearby.

The presence of the *Marblehead* provided just the kind of challenge Stuart gloried in. Here was a perfect opportunity to show his men that the much-vaunted strength of these gunboats was of little use at close range. He demonstrated this in typical fashion.

Gathering together a group of about seventy-five men armed with carbines, Stuart led them across the open ground to attack the gunboat. The *Marblehead* immediately sent ashore a party of sharpshooters to give battle. A brisk skirmish took place. "Our gallant men never faltered in their determination to expose this Yankee bugaboo called gunboat," said Stuart proudly. "To save time, however," he continued, "I ordered up the howitzer, a few shells from which, fired with great accuracy and bursting directly over her decks, caused an instantaneous withdrawal of sharpshooters and precipitate flight under full headway of steam down the river. The howitzer gave chase at a gallop. . . ."

Meanwhile the returning fire of the ship's guns had gone roaring harmlessly over the heads of Pelham's gunners. The little howitzer continued to spit after the fleeing monster gunboat as it steamed down the river in full retreat. Stuart grinned delightedly. The men cheered! They had scared off a *gunboat!*

Leaving the riverbank, the Confederates, in high good humor, turned once more toward the supply depot. As they advanced cautiously into the camp area, they were surprised to find no Union troops at all. The evidence of the enemy's hasty withdrawal lay everywhere. What supplies the Federals had not had time to ship down the river they had set fire to. And, as they left, they had put the torch to Colonel W. H. F. ("Rooney") Lee's home. The famous old White House on the Pamunkey, where George Washington had once courted young Martha Custis, lay in ruins. Stuart was roused to anger by this wanton destruction. He vehemently condemned "the deceitfulness of the enemy's pretended reverence for everything associated with the name of Washington, for the dwelling house was burned to the ground, and not a vestige left except what told of desolation and vandalism."

Moving into the area, the Confederates saw not only the sad remainder of Colonel Lee's plantation house, but such immense piles of burned and partially burned supplies as to make them gape in wonder. Barrels of vinegar had exploded and put out the fires before they had finished their work. Piles of hams, pork shoulders, bacon—all lay partly charred and smoldering. Huge mounds of burned muskets formed hills here and there. Barrel after barrel of salted fish that the fire had never reached lay farther on.

As the Confederates roamed amidst this scene of destruction, they came upon a sight such as hungry soldiers dream about. Before them, laid out as though waiting for a group of Federal soldiers to come forward and buy, was a huge display of sutlers' stores! Fresh fruits, eggs, canned meats, oysters, lobsters, sugar, ice, cakes, candies—"provisions and delicacies of every description lay in heaps," marveled Stuart. The men fell on the food with yells of delight and feasted to repletion. What they could not eat they tried to stuff in pockets, saddlebags, haversacks—anywhere and everywhere they could store their windfall. Men strolled around from one pile of food to the next, eating as they went. Often they had ham or pork shoulders skewered on sabers held jauntily aloft. Even after everyone had his fill there was still so much that many supplies and some equipment were sent back to the Confederate quartermaster at Richmond.

A little later Heros Von Borcke strolled back to the plantation house area. There he found his young commanding officer also taking a break in his usual busy routine. Jeb was stretched out on the ground, leaning back leisurely against one of the many large trees that cast their welcome shade over the plantation yard. He was happily sipping—and enjoying to the utmost—a treat that rarely came the way of a Confederate soldier—a tall glass of lemonade!

General R. E. Lee sent a messenger to ask Stuart what enemy movements he had seen and what he thought McClellan's next move might be. The information Stuart sent back—that there were no signs of retreat from the peninsula and that McClellan was changing his base of operations from the York to the James River—determined in large part the strategy Lee would use in the coming campaign.

Time and again in future situations, Lee was to ask such questions. Time and again he received from Stuart answers that were unusually well informed, intelligent, and accurate. No wonder his commanding officer was to say of Jeb what has been called the highest praise ever given a cavalry officer: "He never brought me a piece of false information."

Meanwhile, far to the rear of Stuart's column, the main Confederate Army, continuing its moves against McClellan, was still having difficulty coordinating its various units. After heavy fighting at Fraysers' Farm and Savage Station, Stuart joined Jackson to pursue the withdrawing Union troops. Once again Pelham's artillery took an active part in the fighting. Since one more of its guns had been rendered useless, the Stuart Horse Artillery had only two little twelve-pound howitzers left. Even with such limited facilities, however, the tactical brilliance of young John Pelham was able to make their fire effective.

During most of this campaign the cavalry, because of orders that it skirt the enemy flank, had not been involved in the major engagements along with the main body of

Lee's army. It was not until July 1 that they were ordered to rejoin the other units.

Jeb was sleeping peacefully when the orders arrived at three-thirty in the morning. He was fully awake and alert at once, as was characteristic of him. Standing next to his bedroll in the darkness was a messenger from General Lee's headquarters. The dispatch he carried said the enemy had been headed off at a road junction. Stuart was ordered to cross the Chickahominy and join Jackson's infantry in order to cover his left flank. In trying to carry out these commands the cavalry found the route they had planned to travel so filled with marching Confederate infantry that they had to backtrack some eleven miles. The whole day turned out to be one of delays and detours.

A few—and brief—rest periods were allowed the men by their hardy young general. One halt was called near a grove of cherry trees loaded with ripe fruit. Immediately the men began to gather the cherries and eat them. Stuart climbed on a fence with the others and, standing on a top rail, enjoyed his share. As the lower branches were soon clean, he called to Von Borcke, "Captain, you charge Yanks so well. Why don't you attack this cherry tree?" Jeb and his staff cheered and laughed as the huge Prussian leaped from the fence and tackled the tree, which broke under his weight. In a few minutes every remaining cherry had been eaten. Then the sound of distant artillery fire was heard. Immediately Jeb ordered "Boots and Saddles!" and they were on their way once more.

When the cavalry finally did get into position on Jackson's left flank, night was already well upon them. There was nothing for them to do but stop and bivouac. The tired troopers climbed thankfully from their saddles. They had ridden forty-two miles that day! They were not too far from the site of the bloody Battle of Malvern Hill, which had been fought that day.

When it was discovered that the enemy had abandoned Malvern Hill during the night, Stuart was sent to reconnoiter the area to see where the withdrawing Federals were concentrating their main strength. Jeb was sure the blue army must be somewhere along the James River. That night he sent Pelham, with his one usable gun, to look for a position from which he could cover the River Road with artillery fire.

Before morning Pelham had sent back exciting news. He had discovered what seemed to be all of McClellan's vast army between Shirley and Westover Plantations. Not only that, but he had also found a long ridge, Evelington Heights, that dominated the whole area. "If we can just get our artillery set up there," said Pelham excitedly, "we can command their entire camping ground!"

Stuart leaped on his horse. Accompanied by Colonel Martin and his brigade of Mississippians, he hurried off to join Pelham at once. What a sight greeted him! Standing on the ridge, he looked down upon hundreds of blue-uniformed soldiers walking about unconcernedly in the camps spread upon the plain that lay between Evelington Heights and the river. What an opportunity this offered! Jeb's deep blue eyes sparkled. Quickly he sent a courier off to give the news to General Lee.

A short time later a messenger returned with word that Longstreet and Jackson were starting forward immediately to give their support. Jeb was delighted. "Now let's see," he thought, "Jackson is only five miles away—that means his troops should start arriving here in about three hours—

fine, we'll start getting ready." At once he had Colonel Martin deploy his men. He ordered Pelham to begin his firing. Of the shelling Stuart said exultantly, "Judging from the great commotion and excitement caused below, it must have had considerable effect."

It certainly told the Grand Army of the Potomac that all was not well. General McClellan himself and most of the other staff officers were absent. General Franklin, who was present, organized his division and began a cautious advance. Slowly and methodically he moved his guns and infantry forward.

Stuart, with only Pelham's one little howitzer and his own handful of men, fought valiantly for five hours. All this time he kept waiting impatiently for the reinforcements. Every minute he expected to hear news of the approach of Longstreet and Jackson. If only he could hold out until they arrived!

At last, sadly, he realized it was no use. When they had fired the last round of ammunition—but not until then—Stuart and the little group were forced to retire from Evelington Heights.

At once Jeb spurred his horse and galloped off at full speed in search of the infantry. When he finally found Longstreet and Jackson, their troops plodding along behind them, he discovered that they had been misdirected by their guides. It was dark before they reached the vicinity of Evelington Heights. Stuart was champing at the bit—attack *now*, he urged! Jackson was against it. He insisted the decision be deferred to Lee.

During the night Federal troops took over Evelington Heights in force. By morning they were firmly entrenched in formidable positions. Union gunboats had steamed forward to cover the flank open to the river. Lee, faced with such a changed situation, decided against an attack. Stuart bemoaned a lost opportunity.

A few days later Jeb's plans fared better. On July 6, accompanied by two regiments of cavalry and Pelham with six guns, Stuart laid an ambush for the Union boats that plied the James with so much self-assurance.

Guns loaded and all in readiness, Stuart hid his men at a landing on the riverbank. They waited in the summer night, excited but quiet, for their unsuspecting prey. Soon five enemy transports hove into sight. Stuart restrained his men until the boats were no more than a hundred yards away. Then "Fire!" he shouted. Pelham's guns roared forth. There was terrific noise as the artillery hit its mark. Von Borcke said, "We could distinctly hear our . . . shells crashing through the sides of the vessels, the cries of the wounded on board, and the confused random commands of the officers."

Amidst the noise that followed, Jeb could make out the sound of gunboats hurrying forward at full steam. Quickly he gathered together his forces. Off they rode in the early summer dawn. Behind them, almost at once, the gunboats turned their artillery upon the exact spot where the Confederates had been only a short while before. Stuart and his staff, turning in their saddles to look back at the scene, laughed as they rode safely away.

It soon became obvious that McClellan was not planning to attack soon. Lee felt the Union forces were harmless where they were. Therefore, on the night of July 8, he withdrew his army and returned to Richmond. Stuart and the cavalry screened this movement and then, on the tenth, they, too, left. Thus ended the Seven Days' Battle.

Jeb wrote Flora:

"I have been marching and fighting for one solid week. Generally on my own hook, with the cavalry detached from the main body. I ran a gunboat from the White House and took possession. What do you think of that?"

From June 26 to July 10, Stuart's cavalry had been engaged continually. They had made several marches of over thirty miles and one of forty-two. The young commander's reputation had grown considerably. Not the least of his exploits in the public mind was his skirmish with the *Marble head*. After all, it was not very often that cavalry could be credited with routing a gunboat!

Largely in recognition for his outstanding services in the Peninsular Campaign, Jeb Stuart was made a major general on July 25, 1862. He was twenty-nine years old.

Chapter VI.

A YANKEE COAT FOR
A CONFEDERATE HAT

THE HANDSOME new major general was now in charge of a cavalry division. Despite the fact that the Confederate Army was becoming—under Lee—somewhat more uniform in its organization, it was still a pretty individualistic affair. Besides the brigades and divisions, there were all sorts of independent units—battalions, legions, etc.

These could be almost any size. A legion or a regiment might be 200 men—or it might be 1000. A brigade might have from two to six regiments. Two brigades—or more— made a division. Regiments were usually made up of local groups; brigades were formed of regiments from the same state. There was no orderly numbering system for the larger units—brigades and divisions were called by the names of their commanding officers.

Stuart's division was at first divided into two brigades. Commanding the first one was Brigadier General Wade Hampton. Hampton, a big, heavy-set man who stood just under six feet tall, was in his early forties. Before the war he had been the wealthiest man in the South and his thoughtfulness, courtesy, and sense of obligation to duty marked him as a Southern gentleman in the fullest sense of that phrase. He had had no military training before the war. It was his intelligence and quick grasp of military situations —as well as his outstanding ability to make men admire and want to follow him—that brought him quickly up the ladder of promotion.

Fitzhugh Lee, whom we have met before, was, like Hampton, a newly promoted brigadier general. He commanded the Second Brigade. Bright and gay, Fitz was only twenty-six years old, but already sported a flowing brown beard reaching almost to his waist. If he hoped this would make him look older he was doomed to disappointment. The face that grinned out from above that fancy chin adornment was still boyish. He enjoyed a joke almost as much as his close friend and former West Point schoolmate, "Beauty" Stuart, did. His military abilities had already been shown to be outstanding.

Stuart got promotions for others among his officers too. Handsome blond Pelham, whose good looks captured the hearts of young ladies wherever he went, became a major. His skill as a master of artillery had spread his renown throughout the South.

Heros Von Borcke, usually dubbed "Von" by his Southern friends, also became a major. Stuart felt the Prussian's energy and enthusiasm in combat had earned this promotion. "Von" wielded a tremendous dragoon sword—no saber for him—said to be the biggest and heaviest in the Confederate Army. It matched his height—he was six feet four—and heft: he was so heavy he had a hard time finding horses that could bear up under his weight.

A pleasant period of inactivity for both the Union and Confederate armies followed the efforts of the Peninsular Campaign. In duty hours Jeb, dressed to the teeth as always when in camp, drilled his men endlessly in cavalry basics. Off duty, the cavalier enjoyed the social activities life in camp permitted.

Mrs. Stuart and the two children—Flora was five now and Jemmie two—were able to be near him once more. Jeb and Flora, as well as other officers of Stuart's staff, were often entertained at the surrounding plantations. On such evenings there was bound to be music—there was always singing when Jeb was around. Flora played the guitar and had a pleasant voice, and of course there was nothing her husband enjoyed as much as letting his golden baritone ring out—unless it was dashing through enemy territory on some dangerous mission. There was dancing, too. Jeb loved to dance and was said to be as expert on the dance floor as on the field of battle.

On a Sunday evening when Stuart and his staff were enjoying just such a social gathering at Dundee Plantation, the cry of "Fire! Fire!" rose from the yard back of the plantation house. Jeb was on his feet at once. He, the other guests, and their hosts streaked around to the rear yard.

Flames poured out of one of the large stable buildings. Instantly Jeb and the other cavalrymen rushed into the burning structure and started carrying out the terrified animals. When all had been safely rescued and the fire put out, the soldiers turned firemen threw themselves on the ground to rest. Throughout the excitement Von Borcke had worked especially hard. Now Jeb looked at him and his big booming laugh rang out as he clapped the big Prussian on the shoulder. In answer to the others' questioning looks,

Jeb—who dearly loved a joke—began declaring that he positively had seen Von come tearing out of the burning stable with two little pigs under one arm and a mule under the other!

Obviously this happy peaceful interlude could not continue. In August the cavalry took part in an engagement at nearby Telegraph Road. When Federals were reported in the vicinity, Stuart led his men quietly through the woods. They were able to move up almost to the road itself unobserved. Jeb, excitement making his blue eyes sparkle, watched the Union soldiers moving confidently along the highway, completely unaware of the hidden gray troopers. Then at the proper moment, Stuart raised his French saber and shouted, "Charge!"

"We fell upon them," he reported exultantly, "like a thunderbolt!"

The Federal infantry fled. Stuart followed this rear guard and fought with it until the main body of troops was forced to stop its forward march to help defend its rear units. Then, his purpose accomplished—and numerous supply wagons, prisoners, and horses captured in the bargain— Stuart withdrew.

Later in the month Jeb went to Orange Court House to consult with General R. E. Lee. He left instructions for Fitz Lee's brigade to move to Verdiersville where he would join it on the seventeenth, the next evening. For some reason these instructions never reached Fitz Lee. The resulting misunderstanding nearly got Stuart captured!

It happened that Fitz Lee's troops were almost out of water and rations. Therefore, without realizing time was important, Fitz Lee leisurely marched his brigade to a nearby Confederate supply depot. There they filled their canteens and haversacks on the seventeenth, pitched camp for the night, and then resumed their march the next day.

Meanwhile Stuart had reached Verdiersville late on the seventeenth. He was surprised not to find Fitz Lee already there and waiting for him. There was not even any word from him. "Fitzhugh," said Jeb to his adjutant, "you go out and meet him; he must be somewhere close by."

Nothing had been heard from the adjutant or Lee by bedtime, so Stuart and his staff settled down for the night on the porch of an old house not far from the road. The sound of horses' hoofs in the distance roused Jeb about daybreak. "There's Fitz now," he thought. Nevertheless, good soldier that he was, he sent out Mosby and Gibson, two of his aides, to check. He himself sauntered out to the front gate. He would be there to meet Fitz Lee when he and his column galloped up. "I might even fuss at him a little, too, for being so late," he thought, grinning to himself.

A second later Mosby and Gibson came flying down the road, spurring their horses to full speed. Bullets whizzed past them. "Yankee cavalry!" they shouted as they pounded by. The Confederate officers scattered. Stuart turned and ran to his horse. Mounting with one huge leap, he dug in his golden spurs. Horse and rider cleared the high back fence in a splendid soaring jump and took off at top speed through the woods.

Von Borcke raced down the road. Hotly pursued, he still managed to outrun his followers. Miraculously the little handful of Confederates all managed to escape. When they met again, after the Federal cavalry had galloped off in the distance, horses and riders alike were out of breath.

Jeb, his hair gleaming red in the August sunshine, was bareheaded. The famous hat was gone! It, his cloak, and haversack—all had been left on the porch in their owner's haste. The passing Federals had picked them up.

Grinning sheepishly, Stuart had a good bit of teasing to take when he and his staff returned to camp. He wrote Flora good-humoredly, "I'm greeted on all sides with congratulations and 'Where's your hat?'" He added, "I intend to make the Yankees pay for that hat!"

Major Fitzhugh had not been so fortunate as his fellow staff officers. He had been captured earlier and was in the Federal camp when the Union raiders returned, one of them wearing the famous plumed hat. Fitzhugh started violently. "Where is the man who wore that hat?" he cried anxiously.

"Oh, he got away," the Federal trooper replied casually.

Fitzhugh breathed a sigh of relief. "Thank God for that!" he said. "That's Jeb Stuart's hat."

The Union soldiers got not only Jeb Stuart's famous hat. They got military information of considerable value—a letter giving a full run-down of Lee's plans against Pope. General Pope was able to move his blue troops before Lee could revise his plans and attack him.

After Pope's move, Jeb asked General R. E. Lee for permission to try to ride around to the rear of Pope's army. Perhaps his railroad communications could be cut at Catlett's Station. This would not only harass the Union troops but embarrass Pope as well, and embarrassing Pope was a popular idea with the Confederates. He had started the practice of seizing prominent Southerners as hostages. He had authorized his soldiers to take whatever they wished from the citizens of Virginia. These practices, coupled with other evidences of what they considered his cruelty and his boasting nature, made General Pope very much disliked by the

Confederates. "Besides," said Jeb with a grin, "I want to make those Yankees pay for my hat!"

In a matter of hours after the order approving the attack on Pope's communications came from Lee, Stuart was ready to go. He took about 1500 men chosen from Fitz Lee's and Robertson's (recently added to Stuart's command) brigades and two of Pelham's guns. As they were riding out of camp Jeb saw Mosby. He waved to him and called out gaily, "I'm going after my hat."

The gray column crossed the Rappahannock and galloped forward unopposed. They were already in the immediate vicinity of Catlett's Station by dark. And it turned out to be a miserable night. The rain fell in torrents. Though Stuart was right where he wanted to be—already amidst the enemy camps—it did not look as though he would be able to do a thing.

It was, Jeb vowed, "the darkest night I ever saw." You couldn't tell friend from foe at ten paces, much less know which way to direct an attack. Luck was with them, however. Through the dark night came the plaintive sound of a voice singing, "Carry Me Back to Old Virginny." When the singer was captured he turned out to be a Negro teamster who had known Stuart in Berkeley County. He recognized Mr. Jeb at once and was glad to see him. Not only that—he knew where General Pope's headquarters were and offered to lead the way to them.

When they reached the camp Stuart sent Blackford, one of his most trusted staff officers, forward to look around. Wearing an oilcloth both as a protection against the rain and to cover his uniform, Blackford rode casually among the tents. He found that the place was practically unguarded. Lights burned brightly in the big tents where the officers were sitting down to bountiful suppers.

Jeb planned his attack. "Rooney" Lee would move against the headquarters camp while the other units destroyed the railroad bridge and created a diversion at the camp next to headquarters. The troopers had to stay close together to maintain contact in the wet pitch-darkness. With the rain covering both the sights and sounds of their movements, they were able to creep in very close before they sprang their trap. Suddenly Jeb ordered the bugles blown. Rebel yells screamed through the darkness as the Confederates leaped forward to attack. Lamps were broken, tables were shoved over, spilling food and dishes in all directions, even tents were pulled down by the Federals as they rushed for cover.

The Confederates took over quickly. Horses, prisoners, and supply wagons were herded together, but it was hard to keep them in the dense downpour. Blackford said afterward, "Panic-stricken by the flashes of lightning and crashes of thunder, the mules stampeded and scattered everywhere. The prisoners slipped through the line of the guard under the horses' bodies and sometimes under their necks, unobserved in the inky blackness of the dark. One flash showed the road full of them, but when another came there would be an empty road."

Unfortunately their attempts to destroy the railroad bridge were in vain. The wet timbers refused to burn. When axes were finally located in the dark night, it was discovered that they were useless on the heavy double beams. Since speed was essential, the attempt to destroy the bridge had to be given up. Stuart gathered his men together and they galloped out before daylight, taking with them over 300 prisoners, numbers of mules and horses, and supply wagons loaded high with captured foodstuffs, baggage, clothing, etc.

When morning came and they stopped to take stock, they found that they had with them Pope's quartermaster and all the Union general's official and personal baggage. Only a lucky chance had kept Pope himself from being captured—he happened to be out of camp on a brief visit.

Jeb chortled with delight when he found amidst their spoil General Pope's most elegant dress uniform coat! Later it was displayed in a shop window on the main street of Richmond for several weeks. Jeb Stuart felt the loss of his hat had been avenged!

Loving a joke as he did, Stuart wrote out a little dispatch to show his friend Stonewall Jackson:

> Major Genl. John Pope
> Commanding, U. S. Army
> General: You have my hat and plume. I have your best coat. I have the honor to propose a cartel for a fair exchange of the prisoners.

Even Jackson laughed.

A courier rushed ahead to take General Pope's captured correspondence to General Robert E. Lee. A valuable find, it gave detailed information as to Pope's projected plans and scheduled army movements.

In his official report of the raid, Stuart said he felt his officers and men deserved "unqualified praise for their good conduct under circumstances where their discipline, fortitude, endurance, and bravery stood such an extraordinary test." He went on to glory in "The horseman, who, at his officer's bidding, without questioning, leaps into unexplored darkness, knowing nothing except that there is a certain danger ahead, possesses the highest attribute of the patriot soldier—It is a great source of pride to me to command such men."

General Pope was not so pleased. He considered the whole affair disgraceful. He also found it embarrassing because, when he had taken over his command, he had spoken out forcefully about the Union Army's concern with routes of withdrawal. "Let us study the probable line of retreat of our *opponents*," he said sternly, "and leave our own to take care of themselves. Let us look before and not behind."

Confederate troopers satirically labeled him "Old-Headquarters-in-the-Saddle," and "The Man without a Rear." His own words came back upon him most humiliatingly. Southern wags even spoke of "Old-Headquarters-in-the-Saddle" as "having his headquarters where his hindquarters ought to be."

And for Pope even more was yet to come. The information in Pope's captured papers made Lee decide that the time to act was now. Pope already had 80,000 men to Lee's 55,000. He must be attacked before McClellan's reinforcements reached him if he was to be attacked at all. With what has been called his "calculated audacity," Lee decided to split his army. He wanted to lure the Union Army away from the Rappahannock to ground of his own choosing.

Accordingly, on August 23 and 24, Stuart's cavalry fought briskly at every possible ford on Pope's front. Longstreet's infantry paraded about in force, making sure that the Union observers across the river saw it. While all this was going on, the forces under Stonewall Jackson quietly withdrew from the river line and began a rapid march northward.

This "foot cavalry" marched twenty-six miles in two days. It was amazing that they could do so, for, as one of ing at once, he sent six companies of cavalry and John Pelham and his guns to hold them off until Jackson could send forward some infantry. Young Patrick—who fell mortally wounded—and Pelham did their work so well that Jackson's infantry was never needed.

That night Stuart and his staff remained ready to spring into action at a moment's notice. They slept near an artillery battery and used the empty shell boxes for pillows. They did not even unsaddle their horses.

The next day the Federals were very slow in moving forward, and when they did, Confederate artillery fire blew great gaps in the long blue lines. At one time during the action Jeb rode to General R. E. Lee to make a report of Federal movements. Lee asked him to wait awhile. General Longstreet reported, astonished by Jeb's coolness, "Stuart turned round in his tracks, lay down on the ground, put a stone under his head and fell instantly asleep."

On Lee's return about an hour later, Jeb was on his feet instantly, fully awake and alert. The commanding general wanted Stuart to send a message to his cavalry. Jeb went himself, leaping on his horse and galloping off singing gaily as he went, "Jine the cavalry!"

Heavy fighting went on until ten o'clock that night, when Pope began his withdrawal. Torrential rains slowed the Confederate pursuit and gave Pope a little breathing spell. He entrenched his forces near Centreville.

Once again the gray troops moved against him. Longstreet attacked his front and Jackson—so well screened by Stuart that Pope did not even know he had withdrawn from his front—moved around his flank. Pope was alarmed to find Confederates behind his right wing. On September 1 he started moving quickly back into the defenses of Alex-

their number said, "Such specters of men they were—gaunt-cheeked and hollow-eyed, hair, beard, clothing, and accouterments covered with dust—only their faces and hands, where mingled soil and sweat streaked and crusted the skin, showing any departure from the whitey-gray uniformity. . . ." The next afternoon they reached Gainesville, where they met Stuart's brigades, who had been doing some notable ground covering themselves. Stuart noted, "I got no sleep, but remained in the saddle all night."

Gainesville was only a few miles from the battlefield of the First Battle of Bull Run or Manassas and it was toward Manassas Junction that the Confederates were heading. A chief objective was the Orange and Alexandria Railroad, the Union Army's life line to Washington. Another goal was the huge Federal depot at Manassas Junction itself.

On Jackson's orders, Stuart placed his cavalry on the front and sides of the infantry and moved toward Bristoe Station. The few enemy pickets there were scattered easily and Confederate soldiers were marching into the area when a long whistle announced the approach of a train. There was not time to block the tracks. The Confederates hurriedly fired their muskets at the passing engine, but it thundered on.

Jackson ordered the switches opened so that the next army trains would race down the embankment to destruction. This was done, but word of the Confederates' whereabouts had already got through, carried by the escaped train. Thus speed became essential. Stuart and Jackson wanted to reach the depot seven miles away before the Federals could burn it to keep the supplies from falling into their hands.

Under cover of night Stuart and his cavalry, accompanied

by two regiments of infantry, hurried off to Manassas Junction, which was easily taken. The rest of the infantry moved up at daybreak.

There followed a time the half-starved soldiers would never forget! After destroying the containers of liquor and securing as much ordnance and public property as could be moved, Stuart and Jackson turned their men loose upon the depot. The infantry—long underfed, lacking shoes, clothes, almost everything (and Stuart's men were in almost as bad a fix)—had a heyday! Von Borcke remembered the scene well: "It was amusing to see here a ragged fellow regaling himself with a box of pickled oysters or potted lobster; there another cutting into a cheese of enormous size . . . while hundreds were opening packages of boots and shoes and other clothing."

They feasted in rare fashion, and what they could not eat on the spot they tried to carry off. Infantry bed and blanket rolls bulged with Yankee delicacies and men marched with hams perched jauntily on the blades of their bayonets. Cavalry troopers one and all rode with a sack of coffee—a rare commodity—lying triumphantly across their saddle horns. Everybody rejoiced in new shoes and clothing, their first in a long, long time.

Federal counterattacks soon began. They were fended off, but Jackson wished to fight on other terrain and so, carrying off what it could and burning what it could not, the army began its withdrawal on the night of August 27. Stuart and his cavalry covered the infantry's flanks and rear as they moved.

The young major general also kept Jackson informed of the enemy's movements. Pope had discovered that Lee had left his front line and so had withdrawn his troops and was

moving them to the Manassas depot, sure that he
Jackson and Stuart there and easily crush them.
arrived, the place was deserted and all was in fl.

Jackson chose his ground and disposed his tr
thickly forested ridge in nearby Groveton. Heav
until 9 P.M. on the twenty-eighth saw the Confe
main in control of the battlefield. All eyes and e
as they waited anxiously for some sign of Longstr
coming to reinforce them. Stonewall sent Jeb o
he could find them. He did and then he briefe
Longstreet as they sat on their horses by the roa
passing infantrymen cheered them as they reco
three generals.

Stuart then went back toward Groveton. Wh
for Longstreet and the infantry to move up—
was a very slow and deliberate sort of person,
hurried—Jeb kept his eye on General Fitz-John
his Union troops. Knowing the Federals far ou
his own column, Stuart decided to try a ruse.
troopers to cutting pine branches from the su
woods. Then, dragging the branches, the gray c
galloped back and forth along the roads, raising
clouds of dust that Porter, sure masses of infa
plodding along those routes, decided the wise t
was to lay low. And this he did, despite Gene
repeated orders to him to go forward.

Meanwhile Stonewall Jackson's forces had pu
six great waves of Union attackers. The Confe
had to fight desperately—one group even used
repel the enemy. At one time during the after
Federal brigades moved around Jackson's flanks
threatening his wagon trains. Jeb saw this mover

andria and Washington. He was completely defeated.

Stuart, who harassed Pope's troops right up to the gates of Washington, got the city's latest papers to send to General Lee. They reported that the defense of the Northern capital had been taken away from Pope and placed in the hands of General George B. McClellan.

Lee, with only 55,000 men at his strongest, had driven an army of 80,000 back some sixty miles, had outmaneuvered it and then outfought it in a pitched battle. The Union Army had lost 13,500 killed and wounded, given up 7000 prisoners and 20,000 rifles, as well as suffering the destruction of a large supply depot. The Confederates had suffered 10,000 casualties. Thus ended the campaign of the Second Battle of Bull Run, or Manassas.

Chapter VII.

SHARPSBURG

AFTER the Confederate victory at Second Manassas, Lee hurriedly began an invasion of Maryland before the Union Army could recover from its defeat. With Stuart and the cavalry covering his movements, he led his army across the Potomac. Neese, a gunner in the Stuart Horse Artillery, noted in his diary, "It was midnight when we left the Southern Confederacy . . . forded the Potomac, and landed in the United States, Montgomery County, Maryland."

The whole thing had a holiday air. Brass bands blared forth at every ford. The strains of "Maryland, My Maryland" filled the air. Many of the men sang and cheered as they waded across the Potomac. The invasion of the North had begun!

At Poolesville, Stuart's first stop in Maryland, the enthusiasm of the local populace was overwhelming. Young men of the town "joined up" with the Confederate Army right and left. Two young merchants who decided to become cavalrymen on the spur of the moment put all their merchandise up for auction. The soldiers found the whole affair a lark. They bid against each other merrily and cleaned out both establishments lock, stock, and barrel, in less than an hour!

Jeb, his staff, and one of his divisions moved on to Urbana, another village stop on their way to Frederick, Maryland. While they were camped there, Stuart, his feet itching to dance, proposed that they give a ball. An old unused academy building on the edge of town was chosen as the site. Von Borcke directed the troopers as they wielded mop and broom to make ready. Local families helped out, and when it was time for the ball to begin the hall was agleam with the light of the many candles and fragrant with the scent of rose garlands.

Young ladies, chaperoned by their families, came from miles around to join the festivities. The band of the 18th Mississippi Infantry opened the evening with "Dixie." The young cavalry officers bowed and escorted their partners to the floor. The silk of the ladies' billowing skirts rustled softly as they moved through the figures of the popular dances of the day.

The ball was in full swing when suddenly a breathless young courier came rushing in. "Yankees! They're attacking!" The word raced around the room. Distant shots could be heard.

Wild confusion followed. Stuart and the other officers rushed from the ballroom and leaped on their horses. Upset mammas and papas gathered together their daughters and herded them toward home.

When the young general reached the scene of action he found that the Federal troops were already starting to retreat. The report had been greatly exaggerated. The Union soldiers were soon completely driven back.

Jeb and the other young cavalry officers were not to be denied their gala evening. Quickly they galloped back to the academy building. The staff officers hurried off to round up the young lady guests and their chaperones once more. In a short time the band had struck up again and the ball was off to another start.

It was still going full tilt at dawn when some of the men wounded in the earlier fighting were brought in. Immediately the scene changed. An impromptu hospital was set

up and the young lady dancers and their mothers set to work as nurses.

Jeb wrote Flora gaily, "The ladies of Maryland make a great fuss over your husband—loading me with bouquets —begging for autographs, buttons, etc. What shall I do?" He loved every minute of it.

Meanwhile General Lee made another of his daring moves. He had hoped that when he crossed the Potomac the Federals would automatically move out of the arsenals at Harpers Ferry and Martinsburg. They had not done so. For the invasion really to get under way these two strongholds to the Confederate rear must be taken. Therefore Lee, even though his army was already less than half the size of the 90,000 troops McClellan had to oppose him, split his own forces. He sent Jackson's corps and three other divisions south to attack the arsenals.

It fell to Stuart and the cavalry to hold open the mountain passes between Harpers Ferry and the main Confederate Army until Jackson could accomplish his mission and move back up to rejoin Lee. This proved to be a more bitter and bloody assignment than was at first thought.

When Lee split his army he was counting on McClellan's slow and overcautious nature to prevent disaster. Fate took a hand against him. In one of the great windfalls of the war, a Union private found, wrapped around three cigars, a copy of Lee's orders to General D. H. Hill. This revealed the scheduled movement of each part of Lee's army.

Even with such information McClellan still delayed, but finally he moved forward in force into the mountain passes. The Confederate infantry, both flanks of which had been turned, moved out under cover of darkness and took up a position at Sharpsburg, along Antietam Creek. Stuart and the cavalry covered them. There was especially bitter fighting at Crampton's Gap and Turner's Gap.

During the fighting in the mountain passes, a civilian with Southern sympathies found out about the lost orders. He rode over to tell the Confederates. When Jeb heard his story he took him to Lee. It was too late to do anything about it, but now they knew what they were up against.

As General McClellan advanced, Stuart slowly retreated, contesting every inch of the ground as he fell back. At one point he delayed the withdrawal of his troops so long that they barely escaped being captured. Finally Harpers Ferry fell to the Confederates and the beleaguered gray troops in the mountain passes could move rapidly toward Sharpsburg.

As the cavalry, hard pressed in their withdrawal, moved through Boonsboro, Colonel "Rooney" Lee's regiment was chosen to make a stand to give the rest of the brigade time to get away. They were steadily pushed back through the town and at one place forced to cross a very narrow bridge with the enemy literally at their heels. As they started to cross the bridge, "Rooney" Lee's horse fell. In a second his own men had come riding down upon him.

One of his captains charged back, pulled Lee's horse to its feet, and shouted to his colonel to climb back on and escape. "Rooney" was too bruised, too stunned and dazed to respond. Before anyone could come closer to help him, another enemy charge came galloping across the bridge. Lee, still stunned and helpless, could only lie on the roadside while the Federal cavalry, then infantry, and finally artillery came thundering by within feet of where he lay.

For some reason nobody noticed him. At last, when he was able to think coherently once more, "Rooney" realized that escape just might be possible. Slowly and painfully he pulled himself along, crawling to the woods that edged the field beside the road. Luck was with him. He met a few Confederate stragglers who carried him to the nearest farmhouse and got a horse for him.

Once on horseback he was able to travel fairly fast. Keeping off the roads, he crossed Antietam Creek before dark and soon was once more back with his friends and fellow cavalrymen. They welcomed him as one returned from the dead!

The news of Jackson's victory at Harpers Ferry had come not one moment too soon for General R. E. Lee. He had only 20,000 men with him on September 14, the day McClellan's army of more than 87,000 stormed the mountain passes. Jackson, by dint of much hard marching, joined Lee on the morning of the sixteenth. Even then the Confederates were greatly outnumbered.

During the fierce and bloody fighting that followed in the Battle of Sharpsburg (or Antietam), Stuart's horse artillery under Pelham and a small body of cavalry held an open hilly area between Jackson's left and the Potomac, a vital spot. As Stuart rode over the battlefield placing his men, his horse had to pick its way carefully over ground so strewn with the dead and wounded there was hardly a place to pass. A road nearby earned its name of "Bloody Lane" that day.

At one point during the day's fighting, Stuart's men had the job of halting, as they moved toward the rear, all the wounded who could walk and carry a gun. Things were so desperate that this group was to be held as a last reserve if the swarms of Federals should break through the front lines. It seemed to some of the cavalry officers that the line was so thin that it would have taken McClellan only one regiment to crash through at any given point. Finally more reinforcements arrived from Harpers Ferry and the war's bloodiest day closed with the Confederate lines restored.

When the expected Union attack did not come the next morning, Lee sent Stuart out to discover why. Jeb learned that large groups of fresh troops were being moved in to support McClellan. Lee decided withdrawal was the wisest course.

Accordingly, Jeb, with Wade Hampton's brigade of cavalry, went galloping out to create a diversion while the main Confederate Army was moving back across the Potomac. On September 19 and 20 Stuart and this small body of men remained on the Maryland side of the river and audaciously sent out small attacking parties against the enemy. Finally the infantry was a safe distance away and Jeb and his men could withdraw to the Virginia side of the river.

For the next six weeks the Confederate troops enjoyed a much-needed rest after the bitter fighting of Sharpsburg. There is a famous story of an incident in which Jeb figured that took place during this little break in hostilities.

It seemed that General Stonewall Jackson, never a person greatly concerned with such worldly affairs as fine clothes, had a uniform coat that had achieved a fame of its own. He had had it since the beginning of the war and had worn it almost constantly. Even when new it had been nothing fancy. Now anyone interested in clothes at all would have considered it a disgrace.

Its original gray color was almost completely lost under a motley of green grass stains, brown and charcoal smudges of campfire soot and gunsmoke, as well as other assorted shades telling of the nights in the field and the hours in rain and dust its wearer had spent. It was torn and frayed and the few buttons it had were plain horn instead of the customary brass.

Major Von Borcke, with a suitable entourage of officers, took a message from Jeb to General Jackson's headquarters. When the official business was completed, Jackson said, "Fine. Now let's have dinner."

"Just a minute, sir," said Von Borcke. "First I have a little gift here from General Stuart, sent with his respects and, I would say, with his love."

An orderly stepped forward with an elaborately wrapped box. Amidst the ohs and ahs of Jackson's staff, Von Borcke drew forth with a flourish a new general's coat. And such a coat! Its fine gray wool faced with soft blue silk, its fire-gilt buttons, its sleeve decorations, stars and wreaths of the most excellent gold embroidery, its fine silk sash, and its snowy gauntlets—truly it was elegance itself!

Jackson obviously was deeply moved. He started saying that it was much too fine to wear and that he would keep it as a souvenir, but his staff would hear of no such thing. Not only did they make him try it on, but they insisted he wear it through dinner too. The word spread through the camp like wildfire. In no time at all hundreds of Jackson's soldiers had come to see. Standing as close as they dared and elbowing each other for a better look, they whispered admiringly.

At cavalry headquarters, now at the Dandridge plantation called the Bower, the soldiers camped under the spreading oak trees that gave the plantation its name. Here they relaxed, hunted, and fished when not on duty protecting the Confederate camps from surprise raids and watching Union troop movements.

The very talented young banjo player, Bob Sweeney, two fiddlers and Jeb's mulatto servant Bob, who "rattled the bones" very well, often supplied music around the campfires or at the dances frequently given at the Dandridge home for the Confederate officers. Thus was enlivened this peaceful interval.

Chapter VIII.

THE CHAMBERSBURG
RAID

As the quiet days went by, the government officials at Richmond began to get a little uneasy. Just what was McClellan up to? What did he have in mind? Lee decided to send Jeb to find out. On October 8 the commanding general issued an order requesting Stuart to ride into Maryland and Pennsylvania, get as much information as to the size, location, and plans of the enemy as he could, cut the railroad line at Chambersburg and damage other transportation as much as possible. He would take 1200 to 1500 men, and the whole affair was to be kept completely secret.

That night General Stuart had his adjutant prepare all the papers he was supposed to look at. Then he closed himself in his tent for two hours, working to clear up all official business. Afterward, everything attended to, he became once more the seemingly carefree cavalier and, to the accompaniment of the banjo, fiddles, and bones, he and some of his fellow officers give their hosts at the Bower a parting serenade.

93

The next morning the cavalry encampment was bustling. Brigadier General Wade Hampton, Colonel "Rooney" Lee, and Colonel William E. ("Grumble") Jones were each in charge of a column of 600 picked men. Major John Pelham commanded the four guns that went along.

When the troopers were assembled, Stuart had a message for them:

"Soldiers! You are about to engage in an enterprise which, to insure success, imperatively demands at your hands coolness, decision, and bravery, implicit obedience to orders without question or cavil; and the strictest order and sobriety on the march and in bivouac. . . ." He also reminded them that, even though horses and other property of U.S. citizens in Pennsylvania subject to legal capture would be taken by the raiding party, plundering by individuals was *absolutely* prohibited. No private property at all was to be seized in Maryland.

The men responded wholeheartedly. Many of them had been with Jeb on his Chickahominy Raid and they had the utmost confidence in him. The secrecy of the mission added to the excitement.

This time McClellan's army lay north of the Potomac between Shepherdstown and Harpers Ferry. Near the ford Stuart planned to use was a Union signal station. Plans were made to surprise the Federal pickets there and capture the station so that word of the Confederates' approach could not be sent out to the rest of McClellan's army.

That night a group of thirty-one hand-picked men led by Lieutenant R. R. Phillips and an experienced guide crept across the river in the darkness. Before daybreak the rest of the column were sitting on their horses at the edge of the ford in dead silence. They were listening for some sound to indicate that Phillips and his men had made their move against the pickets near the signal station. Finally it came, erupting across the tense stillness. The advance guard dashed into the river at once and secured the ford. The rest of the column crossed quickly and quietly.

Once across, they learned that General Cox and some 5000 of his Federal soldiers had passed by only an hour earlier. Soon the advance guard of Stuart's column was so close to the Union troops that they captured ten stragglers. A heavy fog overlay the whole river valley and under its cover the cavalry was able to move so secretly that General Cox continued his march completely unaware that they were behind him.

Though the Union signal station was soon captured, the Federals knew of Stuart's presence north of the Potomac. A local citizen had seen the column splashing across the river at five-thirty that morning and had hurried to tell the military authorities. The whereabouts of the Confederates was reported numerous times before noon, but there was no Union cavalry immediately available. Stuart and his column moved on unopposed.

Although the United States Army knew that Jeb was in the territory, the civilians did not. Even when confronted with the evidence, some of the Pennsylvanians refused to believe that Confederates could be among them. This led to situations the Southerners found very amusing.

In Mercersburg the entire Confederate advance guard was outfitted with new boots and shoes by a merchant who had no idea who they were until they got ready to pay him. Instead of money they gave him legal capture receipts so that he could apply to the Federal government for damages. He was amazed—and no doubt unhappy—to find that he had just presented some six hundred Johnny Rebs with free boots and shoes!

The center section of the column was detailed to collect horses and they spread out on both sides of the road to sweep that section of the Pennsylvania countryside clean. The horses, the huge sturdy work animals used in that area, were excellent for use with artillery though of no value for cavalry mounts. Many of the Pennsylvania farmers thought it was the Federal army that was impressing their horses. They would launch into a tirade against Abe Lincoln and the government at Washington. When they had finished, the Confederate cavalryman, grinning from ear to ear, would say he could not agree more. Then he would tell the astonished farmer who he was and gallop off leading the captured horses. With typical gallantry, Stuart gave orders that the horses of ladies not be taken, but that they be allowed to ride by undisturbed.

Chambersburg was occupied on the night of October 10. Stuart's excellent control over his men was shown in their exemplary behavior in that town. Many of the citizens of the town—all Union sympathizers—were so impressed that they voluntarily expressed their admiration and appreciation.

One of them, Colonel McClure, later owner of the Philadelphia *Times*, wrote of the officers he met, "Most of them were men of more than ordinary intelligence and culture, and their demeanor was in all respects eminently courteous." Of both enlisted men and officers he went on to say, "All, however, politely asked permission to enter the house, and behaved with entire propriety. They did not make a single rude or profane remark even to the servants."

They requested Colonel McClure to serve them. They ate

much of his food, drank all his coffee and then went on to drink all his tea, but they did it like gentlemen. They took all his best tobacco, too, but asked his permission to smoke! Colonel McClure reported, "I was somewhat bewildered by this uniform courtesy. . . ."

Though private plundering was forbidden, the soldiers had a heyday when the government depot was opened. A Pennsylvania newspaper reporter described the scene:

"The whole town was converted into one vast dressing room. On every hotel porch, at every corner, on the greater portion of the street doorsteps, might be seen Rebel cavalry donning Yankee uniforms, and throwing their own worn-out and faded garments into the street. Each took as many coats, hats, and pairs of pants as he could conveniently handle."

A party of Confederates sent out from Chambersburg to destroy the railroad bridge, a prime objective of the raiders, had to admit failure. The bridge was made of iron and all of their attempts against it proved futile.

That night there was a steady downpour. Stuart, bivouacked with his staff on the outskirts of Chambersburg, could not sleep. It was rare indeed for him to show worry, but it was obvious he was concerned. Three times he woke Captain B. S. White, his principal guide for the trip back, to ask him if the heavy rains would raise the river to uncrossable heights. Each time White assured him that they could easily beat the floodwaters to the lower fords. Still Stuart worried and paced back and forth. He knew that the Union cavalry must be even then gathering its forces to close in on him and trap his column. Usually he could sleep easily under the most trying circumstances, but he did not sleep that night.

Finally the long night was over. The men mounted their horses and the column set off in the direction of Gettysburg. Once more Stuart had decided that the boldest action was his safest course. He was going to ride around McClellan's army again!

As they trotted along, Jeb, riding at the head of the main body of his troops, called Captain Blackford forward. For several minutes after his engineer officer joined him the young general remained silent. Then he said, "Blackford, I want to explain to you my reasons for selecting this route for return; and if I do not survive, I want you to vindicate my memory."

He pulled out his map. "You see, the enemy will be sure to think that I will try to recross above, because it is nearer to me and farther from them. They will have all the fords strongly guarded in that direction, and scouting parties will be on the lookout for our approach so that they can concentrate to meet us at any point. They will never expect me to move three times the distance and cross at a ford below them and so close to their main body, and therefore they will not be prepared to meet us down there.

"Now, do you understand what I mean? And don't you think I am right?"

Blackford assured him that he did and that, if need be, he would pass those reasons on to others.

Meanwhile the whole Federal Army had been alerted by midnight of October 10. They knew the Confederates were at Chambersburg that night, but McClellan wisely waited to see where Stuart was heading next before sending his cavalry out after him. Meanwhile he took every step he could think of to make sure the Confederates didn't escape. He reported to Washington:

I have made such disposition of troops along the river that I think we will intercept the Rebels in their return. All of my available cavalry was ordered in pursuit last night, but as yet nothing has been heard from it.

Cox's division is loaded in cars at Hancock, with cavalry well out toward the Pennsylvania line, and if the Rebels attempt to cross below Hancock, I have infantry at or near all the different fords.

I have six regiments of cavalry now up the river between Hancock and Cumberland. All of these troops have been ordered to keep a sharp lookout for the return of the Rebels. . . .

I have given every order necessary to insure the capture or destruction of these forces, and I hope we may be able to teach them a lesson they will not soon forget.

All the Union signal stations had been alerted. Two infantry divisions had been loaded into railroad cars and the engines waited, steamed up, to take off in any direction at a moment's notice. McClellan was sure he had Stuart this time!

The weather was on Stuart's side—a fog obscured the movements of the gray column all morning. Besides that, the Federal cavalry under General Pleasonton had not been ordered out until the eleventh and then had lost two hours following a false lead. At last, at midnight, he did find out where Stuart was and set out at once to follow. When, by dint of much hard and fast traveling—seventy-eight miles in twenty-eight hours—they finally came within striking distance, so many of his men had straggled behind that Pleasonton did not have enough vigorous troops left to be effective.

Meanwhile Stuart was better informed than Pleasonton.

The papers carried by a captured courier had told him of Federal troop concentrations and movements. The gray column plunged on without rest. The men switched mounts, riding captured horses to rest their own. It was the only way they could keep up the terrific pace. Some of them gathered green corn from the fields as they rode by and fed their horses as they trotted along. Just before dark they reached Emmitsburg. The Confederates were happy to be with the friendly people of Maryland again. They, in turn, were surprised indeed to see the gray column. Captain Blackford was amused to find that "If we had fallen from the clouds the people could not have been more astonished than at seeing us come from the direction we followed. . . ."

The friendly Marylanders brought out food, which the hungry and grateful soldiers gulped on horseback. The dispatches captured from the courier showed Jeb that their route must be changed and an all-night ride was essential—there was no time for a leisurely meal.

The all-night march was something Stuart and his men never forgot. Captain Blackford said later: "It is no small tax upon one's endurance to remain marching all night; during the day there is always something to attract the attention and amuse, but at night there is nothing. The monotonous jingle of arms and accoutrements mingles with the tramp of horses' feet into a drowsy hum all along the marching column, which makes one extremely sleepy, and to be sleepy and not to be allowed to sleep is exquisite torture. . . . Many of the men went fast to sleep on their horses and snores loud and long could be heard all along the column."

By daylight on October 12 the Confederates had reached Hyattstown. Incredibly, Jeb had gathered some of his staff and gaily taken a quick dash down to spend a brief half hour with friends near Urbana, as though war were a million miles away! He rejoined the column at Hyattstown as they began covering the last twelve miles that lay between them and safety.

It was now that Captain B. S. White performed his invaluable service as guide. He had been born in the area and knew every little country road. It was in large part due to him that the column was able to get through safely.

All about them now Union troops were moving. Three brigades of infantry, supported by cavalry, guarded all the lower fords of the Potomac. The Federals were closing in from all sides. Capture appeared almost certain.

General Pleasonton and his men—two artillery pieces and 400 cavalry were all that had been able to keep up the killing pace—were on their way to Poolesville, Maryland. The Confederate advance guard under Fitz Lee appeared suddenly out of the dense wood through which they had been traveling. As they did, the Federal cavalry came into view trotting down the highway. Pleasonton and Stuart were using the same road!

Now it happened that the October morning was chilly. The Confederate troops still wore their overcoats—new blue ones they had acquired at the Chambersburg depot. The whole countryside was filled with Union troops hunting for the raiders. Pleasonton could not be sure at first glance whether these were fellow Federals or not.

Jeb, trotting along at the head of the advance guard, saw their hesitation. He lifted his hand. "Hold off, men," he told his troops; "let's wait."

The Federal cavalry continued their approach. They even thought the restraining gesture of Stuart's hand had been a friendly greeting! When they were quite close Stuart gave the order "Draw sabers! Charge!" Immediately the Confederate cavalry, making the morning air ring with the Rebel yell, came galloping down upon the surprised Federals. The front lines of blue troopers were knocked off the road by the force of the charge and were driven back upon their main body. Immediately Pelham and his guns came galloping forward. The Union cavalrymen scattered almost at once. Pleasonton was so sure that Stuart was going to try to cross the Potomac at the mouth of the Monocracy that he felt he could wait for reinforcements before he renewed his attack. He decided to sit back until the infantry and artillery could move up to help him.

This decision gave Stuart two more hours—and that was all he needed. While he, Pelham, and the rear guard remained behind to fend off Pleasonton, "Rooney" Lee and the advance guard moved on to White's Ford. What they saw when they arrived made their hearts stand still—Federal infantry lined the bluffs commanding the ford!

The situation looked desperate to Lee. The Union troops were well entrenched and had full coverage of the river crossing. He sent for Stuart to come and look the situation over himself. "Sorry," Jeb replied, "I've got my hands full here" (the rear guard had been attacked); "the ford must be taken—at hazards."

There was nothing left for Lee to do but attack. He set about plotting his strategy: send parties to attack the bluff from the front and left simultaneously while another group of cavalrymen tried to rush across the ford under enemy fire . . . hope one piece of artillery might make it across and then turn its fire upon the Federal rear. It looked as though the chances for success were very slim indeed, but "the ford must be taken—at hazards!' "

Lee set about getting his troops ready for the attack. Then he thought he might try a little subterfuge.

He sent a courier, handkerchief waving from his saber, with a message for the Union commander. The note told him that General Stuart's whole command confronted him and that the hopelessness of the Union situation must be obvious. Lee requested him to surrender in order to avoid unnecessary bloodshed—he had fifteen minutes to decide.

That fifteeen minutes seemed to last forever. The Confederate troopers sat on their horses in nail-biting silence. The line of gray cavalry filed out to the left flank, ready to attack. There was no sign of surrender from the Federals.

The time was up. Oh well, thought "Rooney," you couldn't really expect it to work. He turned and gave the command "Fire!" The artillery opened up. Any minute now the returning fire of the enemy would be booming forth.

Then shouts rang out from the Confederate lines: "Is it possible? They are retreating! Retreating!" The gray troopers could not believe their eyes—but it was true! There went the Federal infantry, abandoning their strong position without firing a shot. A long ragged cheer rose from Confederate throats—safety was in sight!

The main body had reached the river by this time. Pelham hurried his artillery across. They quickly got set up, ready to cover the crossing. The prisoners, the led horses, the main body of Confederate cavalry splashed across to safety. Where was the rear guard? Blue troops could be seen moving forward on the distant hills. Where was that rear guard? Four couriers had been sent back to hurry Colonel Butler and his men with no results.

Stuart, his emotion obvious, spoke to Captain Blackford at the edge of the ford. His voice shook.

"Blackford, we are going to lose our rear guard!"

"How is that, General?"

"Why, I have sent four couriers to Butler, and he is not here yet; and see—there is the enemy closing in behind us!"

"Let me try it!" cried Blackford.

Jeb hesitated. Then he extended his hand. "All right," he said, "and if we don't meet again—good-by, old fellow!"

In a second Blackford was splashing across the ford. He rode furiously and galloped past all four couriers sent searching for Butler earlier. When he reached the rear guard he found it hard pressed as it fended off enemy forces. Blackford dashed up breathlessly. "General Stuart says, 'Withdraw at a gallop or you will be cut off!'"

Butler replied with the calm courage so characteristic of him, "But I don't think I can bring off that gun. The horses can't move it."

"Leave the gun," said Blackford, reining his impatient horse, "and save your men!"

"We'll see," said Butler.

This time—to everyone's surprise—the exhausted horses responded. The gun leaped out of the mudhole. Off it went, Butler and his men galloping down the road behind it. Federal bullets and artillery shells whizzed by them as they went. In a few minutes they were splashing madly across the Potomac and the whole column was soon safe on Virginia soil. Had they waited even ten more minutes, the entire rear guard would probably have been lost.

The pursuing enemy stopped at the river. Pelham's guns fired a few shots at them, but they made no attempt to follow.

The long gray column halted for a few minutes to catch their breath and then trotted on the ten miles to Leesburg. There they tumbled from their horses for their first real sleep in days. They had made a remarkable march from Chambersburg—eighty miles in twenty-seven hours. This was even more remarkable when one considered that they were slowed down by the artillery and the large numbers of led horses they had with them. The only casualty was one man wounded. Two men, who for some reason had dropped out of line, had been captured.

Federal authorities at Chambersburg estimated the value of the public and railroad property the Confederates had destroyed there at $250,000. A large number of horses—it has been estimated at 1200—had been taken. Thirty prominent citizens had been captured to be held as hostages for the Virginia citizens the United States had seized. The only important objective the expedition had not been able to accomplish was the destruction of the iron railroad bridge.

One loss on the expedition was not mentioned in any of the official records. Stuart's servant, Bob, partaking of too much of the apple cider in abundance in the Pennsylvania apple country in October, had fallen asleep by the roadside. He was captured and with him two of Jeb's special horses, Skylark and Lady Margrave, a real loss to the young cavalryman.

Stuart's exploit once more shook Union morale, both civilian and military. Another result of the raid was the delay of a Federal attack. McClellan had been ordered on October 6 "to cross the river and attack the enemy." He says in his report that his having used all his cavalry against Stuart had quite an effect—"this exhausting service completely broke down nearly all of our cavalry horses and rendered a remount absolutely indispensable before we could advance on the enemy."

Stuart's contemporary biographer thought one of the principal causes of the success of the remarkable expedition was the fact that Stuart was always present at the time and place of danger. He says, "He habitually rode with his advance guard, and was ever ready to seize and improve an opportunity. He could 'trust in Providence' with an honest and sincere faith: but he also *kept his powder dry*."

Chapter IX.

THE FALL
OF THE GALLANT

AFTER the hard riding and fighting on the Chambersburg Raid, Stuart and the cavalry got only two days' rest upon their return. After that there was a period of almost constant fighting. McClellan and his army began moving south and the cavalry was called upon to fight a delaying action. It fought hard as it fell back inch by inch, forced to give ground before far superior forces.

It was during this almost daily fighting that Jeb received an urgent call to visit his little daughter Flora. She had been seriously ill for some time and now Mrs. Stuart wrote her husband begging him urgently to take leave to come home to see her.

Her message reached him on the battlefield. He wrote back,

> I was at no loss to decide that it was my duty to you and Flora to remain here. I am entrusted with the conduct of affairs, the issue of which will affect you, her, and the mothers and children of our whole

country much more seriously than we can believe.

If my darling's case is hopeless, there are ten chances to one that I will get to Lynchburg too late; if she is convalescent, why should my presence be necessary? Let us trust in the good God who has blessed us so much, that He will spare our child to us, but if it should please Him to take her from us, let us bear it with Christian fortitude and resignation.

When, a few days later, the telegram telling of the little girl's death arrived, Jeb was completely overcome. Many nights thereafter, his aides would see their general, his orders issued and all his paper work taken care of, bow his head upon his arms, his broad shoulders shaking with the anguish of his loss. But he kept his grief private, and he rode before his division with his bearing as proud and military as ever. He wrote tender, grieving letters to his wife. A year later, on the Gettysburg campaign, he sent her blue cornflowers —they reminded him of little Flora's eyes.

Mrs. Stuart and Jemmie, three years old, came for a short visit to Jeb's headquarters after little Flora's death, so the grieving family could comfort one another. An orderly was assigned to keep track of little Jemmie, who was brimming over with energy and enthusiasm. He reminded everyone of his handsome father, and it was said the whole cavalry spoiled him.

Summarizing this period of the cavalry's delaying action, Stuart praised "the gallant and patient endurance of the cavalry, fighting every day most unequal conflicts, and successfully opposing for an extraordinary period the onward march of McClellan." He went on to say, "The Stuart Horse Artillery comes in for a full share of this praise, and its gallant commander, Major John Pelham, exhibited a skill and courage which I have never seen surpassed. . . . I was more than ever struck with that extraordinary coolness and mastery of the situation which more eminently characterized this youthful officer than any other artillerist who has attracted my attention. . . ."

On November 7, General McClellan was replaced by General Burnside as commander of the Army of the Potomac. When Burnside moved the Union troops down the Rappahannock, Lee moved to oppose him, entrenching his forces around the city of Fredericksburg. While the two armies were getting ready for action there was a more or less quiet period. It happened that in those late November days there were several heavy snowfalls. The Confederates, to many of whom so much snow was a novelty, had some enthusiastic snowball fights. The officers led their men in furious charges and countercharges. One onslaught took place near Stuart's headquarters. The air was white with snowballs. Stuart stood on a box and cheered the participants on as the battle line moved back and forth. All too soon the Confederates turned from these pretend battles to the real thing.

The woods and hills of the battlefield of Fredericksburg made it impossible for the cavalry to take a very large part in the fierce fighting there. The horse artillery, however, was given an opportunity and performed spectacularly. When Jeb gave the order to the artillery to open fire, Pelham asked permission to rush two guns forward. That way he could start shooting long before the whole battery could advance and go into action. Stuart consented and Pelham led the way onto the open field. In a few minutes one artillery piece was rendered useless by enemy fire, but the other, a trusty Napoleon, continued to roar forth. The cross fire from this one gun of Pelham's halted the Federal advance for over an hour. Though some thirty-two enemy cannon focused their fire upon him, Pelham held his position and continued to shoot. So many of the gun crew were killed that the young major himself helped load and fire the gun. It was only when his ammunition was exhausted that Pelham gave the order to return to his battery. Generals Lee and Jackson had seen this exchange and both were warm in their praise of the young Alabamian. Meeting Stuart later, Stonewall said, "Have you another Pelham, General? If so, I wish you would give him to me!"

The Southern victory at Fredericksburg left the hills blue with dead. The Federals lost some 13,000 men to the Confederates' 5000, though two Southern generals had been killed in the fierce fighting. The city of Fredericksburg itself, its ground plowed by cannon and littered with bodies, lay in ruins.

Soon after his withdrawal from Fredericksburg, General Burnside began to settle into winter quarters. Learning this from Jeb's ever watchful cavalry, Lee and his troops set up winter quarters on the south side of the river across from the Federals. The gray infantry gratefully enjoyed this small vacation from constant marching and fighting.

The cavalry, however, was not so fortunate. Upon its constant watchfulness depended the safety of the whole army. Reconnaissance, guarding of the Rappahannock fords, and raids to the rear of Burnside's army kept it busy. On one of these expeditions, the famous Dumfries Raid, Stuart reacted characteristically when his forces surprised a Union telegraph operator before he could give the alarm. Stuart put his own telegraph operator on the key and was soon receiving official information directly from Washington giving the troop movements that were being made to stop the Confederate raiders. Then Jeb, always fond of a joke, had his operator send a message to the Union quartermaster general at Washington:

> I am much dissatisfied with the transport of mules lately sent which I have taken possession of, and request that you send me a new supply.
>
> J. E. B. Stuart

Now, of course, Washington knew his whereabouts, so Jeb had the telegraph wires cut and moved quickly on his way. As a result of the raid, the Federals lost over two hundred men and some twenty wagons and sutlers' teams; Stuart had one man killed, thirteen wounded, and fourteen missing.

This winter was a period of intense hardship for the Confederates. They lacked clothes, shoes, food—almost every necessity. The cavalry horses were underfed, gaunt and sick, with many dying. The Federal troops on the other hand were receiving new supplies and equipment—the best money could buy—every day. Under their new general— "Fighting Joe" Hooker had replaced Burnside—they were being reorganized and strengthened. This was particularly true of the Union cavalry, which was never again to be the easy mark it had been in the early part of the war.

With the beginning of spring came increased activity between the two armies. On March 17, 1863, there took place an engagement often called the first of the battles between the Union and Confederate cavalry. The Union cavalry had ventured so far south that they could not depend on their infantry and the battle was fought almost entirely on horseback. Brigadier General Averell and a large body of

Union cavalry moved south "to attack and rout or destroy" Fitz Lee's brigade near Culpeper Court House. On March 17, 1863, fierce fighting took place as Averell pushed across the Rappahannock at Kelly's Ford and ran into Fitz Lee's force charging up the road to meet him. The battle raged on with charges and countercharges; though Fitz Lee had only 800 men to Averell's 2100, neither side seemed able to gain any material advantage over the other.

Meanwhile Jeb and John Pelham had been attending a court-martial at Culpeper Court House. They were supposed to have gone back to Fredericksburg on the seventeenth, but when they heard of the enemy attack they borrowed horses and went galloping off to the scene of action.

Soon after they arrived one Confederate regiment broke and ran after receiving murderous fire from behind the stone fence they had charged. Instantly Stuart was among them, waving his big plumed hat and yelling to them to stay with him and charge again. One of the officers of the regiment said in admiration, "Never did I see one bear himself more nobly. I stopped to gaze on him, though I expected every moment to hear the dull *thud* of a bullet and see him fall."

The fighting soon covered the field. Jeb's saber flashed and clashed as he fought and rode wherever the action was fiercest. Fitz Lee, who had two horses shot out from under him, was also constantly in the thick of things.

Meanwhile Pelham had gone to help Major James Breathed find a good location for his guns. Federal shells flew thick and fast around them. When the 3rd Virginia Regiment got ready to charge the Federal troopers entrenched behind the stone fence, Pelham joined them. He had no artillery to command and couldn't bear to be out of the action. Suddenly as the line surged forward, an officer cried out, "My God, they've killed poor Pelham!"

Pelham's riderless horse went on and there lay the handsome young major, as one who was there said, "on his back, his eyes open, and looking very natural." He never regained consciousness. When they told Jeb what had happened he bowed his head upon his horse's neck and wept unashamed. Blackford said of Pelham, "Stuart loved him like a younger brother and could not bear for him to be away from him." Stuart's commemorative order to his cavalry shows his love and admiration, as well as his sense of loss:

"The noble, the chivalric, the gallant Pelham is no more. How much he was beloved, appreciated, and admired, let the tears of agony we here shed, and the gloom of mourning throughout my command bear witness. His loss is irreparable. . . . His record has been bright and spotless, his career brilliant and successful. He fell, the noblest of sacrifices, on the altar of his country. . . ."

People came in crowds to lay flowers on Pelham's casket as his body was borne home to Alabama. Three young ladies of Virginia put on mourning for him.

The Battle of Kelly's Ford had lasted from five in the morning to five in the afternoon. Averell, despite his having 2100 men and six guns to Fitz Lee's 800 men and four guns, had been able to advance less than two miles toward his objective, Culpeper Court House. He lost eighty men. Fitz Lee counted eleven killed, eighty-eight wounded, and thirty-four captured. But how to estimate the immeasurable loss of Pelham?

Chapter X.

CHANCELLORSVILLE

By EARLY 1863 raids, picket duty, and the almost constant skirmishing that accompanied them had left Stuart's cavalry greatly weakened. Suitable horses were at a premium and their dwindling numbers were a great problem. Horseshoes and nails were hard to come by, too, and the effectiveness of the cavalry suffered from these deficiencies as well as from the poor quality of all their equipment and weapons. Each Confederate cavalryman owned his own horse and when something happened to that horse it was his responsibility—and expense—to get another one. This made absenteeism a constant problem. Often half the cavalry force was away—men were always having to go home to get new mounts. Conditions, bad enough in the Virginia regiments, were far worse in Wade Hampton's brigade, where the men had to make their way home to South Carolina, North Carolina, Georgia, or even Mississippi to get their remounts!

In contrast, the Union cavalry was in better condition than it had ever been. Now a single corps under Major General George Stoneman, it was outfitted with the latest, newest, and best equipment, as well as the finest horses available. He had 12,000 men and 13,000 horses in his command.

In early April there were skirmishes between the two groups of cavalry as Stoneman pressed southward to prepare the way for the major advance of the Union Army under General Hooker. On the afternoon of April 28 a strong group of Federals crossed the Rappahannock in boats and built a pontoon bridge. During the night two entire corps of the Union Army crossed the river. At once Stuart, ever alert, sent word to Robert E. Lee of this movement. He was ordered to swing around the Federal troops and join Lee at Fredericksburg. He did so, fighting a delaying action as he went.

Hooker continued moving his forces forward. By the night of April 30 he had his whole army south of the Rappahannock. This had been accomplished with very few losses and almost no real fighting. Hooker thought the situation looked very bright indeed.

Meanwhile Lee had sent some troops out from Fredericksburg toward Chancellorsville. Chancellorsville was not a town, but a large manor house with its various outbuildings. Between it and Fredericksburg the countryside was fairly open, but on the other three sides it was surrounded by dense forest and underbrush. This "wilderness," as it was called, was about fifteen miles wide and twenty miles long. Two good roads crossed this area—the Plank Road and the Old Turnpike.

On the night of May Day, Stuart galloped up to army headquarters. He brought Lee and Jackson news that Hooker, though well fortified on the south, southwest, and east at Chancellorsville, had no defenses on the west or north. Another piece of valuable information the young general brought concerned the discovery of an old, little-used wagon road circling around Hooker's army.

Lee and Jackson decided to act at once. Jackson would move quickly down this road and fall upon Hooker's rear the next day. Their chances of defeating Hooker's huge army appeared slim indeed but this plan seemed to offer some slight glimmer of hope. Though the withdrawal of Jackson's corps would leave Lee with only 14,000 men to face Hooker's 100,000, the commanding general did not hesitate a second to approve the movement.

Early the next morning Jackson set out with Stuart's cavalry screening his departure. When Stonewall's whole corps started their march—directly south at first—Federal scouts spying from the tops of the tallest pine trees jubilantly called down the news that Lee's army was in full retreat! Soon the Confederates, having swung westward and being completely hidden from view by the dense forest, were marching rapidly down the old cart road.

Fitz Lee and his cavalry, who were moving ahead of Jackson, had reached the Plank Road and were waiting for the infantry to catch up. While he was waiting Fitz Lee decided to do a little personal looking around. The Federal lines proved surprisingly close. The Union troops had no idea the Confederates could reach the road at this place and there were no bluejacket guards posted anywhere near Fitz Lee's vantage point. Fitz looked down on the peaceful scene: "Below, and but a few hundred yards distant, ran the Federal line of battle. . . . The soldiers were in groups in the rear, laughing, chatting, smoking; probably engaged, here and there, in games of cards, or other amusements indulged in when feeling safe or comfortable, awaiting orders. . . ."

Jackson immediately had his troops take up positions on the turnpike. Before six that evening everything was ready. The attack surged forward, the long wild Rebel yell ringing out as the line swooped down upon the unsuspecting enemy, many of whom were peacefully cooking their supper. Here and there little islands of blue soldiers stood their ground and fought bravely, but soon had to give way as they were surrounded. Soon the whole Federal corps turned and fled, a disorganized mass.

The Confederates pursued. In the darkness that had now fallen they had to stop and reform their lines. Jackson ordered A. P. Hill's division, which had been in the rear, to ride through the troops and take over the front lines. Meanwhile Stonewall and some of his staff rode forward for a closer look at the Federal dispositions. Union troopers fired on them and they turned and rode quickly back toward their own lines. At this moment Hill's forces were moving up. They did not know their general was in front of their lines and when they saw a group of horsemen come dashing toward them in the darkness, they fired on them. Two men fell dead at their first volley. The second volley hit General Jackson, who fell wounded in three places. Stonewall, in great pain, was finally taken to the field hospital. At midnight his left arm was amputated at the shoulder.

Meanwhile Stuart, having found little use for his cavalry on the main battlefield, had asked Stonewall for permission to hold the road to Ely's Ford. He was getting ready to attack the Union troops he had found there when word came that both Jackson and A. P. Hill had been wounded and that he was to have command of Jackson's corps.

One cavalry regiment was already drawn up in battle line. Quickly Jeb told one of his officers his plan of attack and gave the first orders. Then, without waiting to see how things would turn out, he spurred his horse and galloped off in the night to his new duties.

Jeb had to assume those duties under difficult circumstances. He had no idea what Stonewall's plans of attack were. When Stuart asked for suggestions, Jackson replied, "Tell General Stuart to act upon his own judgment and do what he thinks best; I have implicit confidence in him." This must have been very gratifying to Jeb, but it was not much help!

Stuart was not familiar with the terrain over which they were fighting nor did he know the disposition of any of the forces. Only one of Jackson's staff reported to him. Worst of all, it had been impossible to hide the fact that Jackson had been wounded and the word had run like wildfire throughout his command. His troops were greatly upset and the effect of this disastrous news upon them was apparent.

Stonewall's various subordinate commanders reported the positions of their troops to Stuart. Since it was evident that Jackson had confided his plan of attack to no one, Jeb decided to wait till morning to press forward.

During the rest of the night Stuart worked hard, getting acquainted with the terrain and the disposition of troops. A reconnaissance report from a scout he had sent out showed that the key Federal position was Hazel Grove, a ridge on which the Union artillery was posted in strength. Accordingly Jeb made that spot a chief target for his attack.

The furious battle began at dawn. Along the Plank Road the two lines of infantry stood steady, facing each other and pouring a constant hail of fire at each other's lines for hours. On the Confederate left the line swayed back and forth with the various charges and countercharges. It was on the Confederate right that the decisive fighting took place, however. Brigades from various gray divisions united to attack the strong Union position on Hazel Grove and finally, after much furious fighting, the ridge was taken.

Jeb then posted thirty artillery pieces on Hazel Grove and the fight moved on into the clearing beyond. Covered by this artillery fire, the Confederate lines advanced. Stuart himself led two of the charges. As he galloped along at the head of the attacking forces, his golden voice could be heard ringing clear above the clamor of the battlefield: "Old Joe Hooker, won't you come out of the Wilderness?" The sight of this singing cavalier leading the way into battle created a great surge of enthusiasm among Jackson's troops. As Jeb rode conspicuous into the fray, French saber held on high and dark plume and scarlet-lined cape blowing, one of the officers said he "looked like a very god of battle."

While Stuart was attacking on the west, General Lee's forces, under Dick Anderson, were moving forward on the east and south to join Jackson's corps. The third assault on the entrenched Federal line was successful and Anderson and Stuart joined forces, sweeping the whole Union Army before them. The battle was won.

General E. P. Alexander, whose own military abilities lend weight to his opinion, said, "Altogether, I do not think there was a more brilliant thing done in the war than Stuart's extricating that command from the extremely critical position in which he found it as promptly and as boldly as he did. . . . He decided to attack at daybreak; and, unlike many planned attacks that I have seen, this one came off promptly on time, and it never stopped to draw its breath until it had crashed through everything and our forces stood united around Chancellor's burning house. . . .

"That Sunday morning's action ought to rank with whatever else of special brilliancy can be found in the annals of
the Army of Northern Virginia; and as a test of the mettle
of a commander it would be hard to conceive severer demands or more satisfactory results."

Even the enemy commented upon Stuart's bravery and
daring in his one infantry command. A Federal officer,
Colonel W. L. Goldsmith, described Stuart's charge into
battle as "the bravest act I ever saw."

Once the whole Union Army had retired to the other
side of the Rappahannock, the command of Jackson's corps
was turned over to A. P. Hill. Stuart, his first and only big
infantry command eminently successful, returned to his
own cavalry command. When told later that the dying
Jackson had requested that Stuart take over his command,
Jeb said, "I would rather know that Jackson said that than
to have the appointment."

Chancellorsville had cost both sides heavily. The Federals
had lost more than 11,000 killed and wounded and 6000
prisoners; the Confederates more than 10,000 killed and
wounded and close to 2000 prisoners. The reckoning of
Southern losses must include something else—on May 10,
1863, Thomas Jonathan ("Stonewall") Jackson died. After
calling in his delirium for A. P. Hill to come up—an echo
of the last order he gave on the battlefield—he sank back,
no longer delirious, but peaceful and calm, and said, "Let
us pass over the river and rest under the shade of the trees."
The Confederate Army had lost a military genius and Jeb
Stuart had lost a dear friend.

Chapter XI.

THE BATTLE
OF BRANDY STATION

AFTER the Confederate victory at Chancellorsville, Stuart's cavalry once more had a short period of rest. Many recruits had arrived with fresh horses and Jeb had almost 10,000 cavalrymen in his command, the most he had ever had. This, plus the fact that the summer grass was green and plentiful and both men and horses for the moment adequately fed, seemed cause for celebration. Jeb had always enjoyed the color, glory, pomp and circumstance of military reviews—especially if there was an audience to appreciate it. Now he decided to hold a special review to show General Lee and the other commanders the splendor of his cavalry troops.

On June 5, a day of brilliant sunshine and high pageantry, the review was held. General Lee, it turned out, could not be present. There was a large crowd there, however. The local populace, as well as visitors from as far away as Richmond, turned out to gaze admiringly at the 9000 cavalrymen who rode by, first at a walk and then at a gallop. The guns of the artillery battalion on a hill across from the spectator's stand belched forth brilliant flame and black smoke. The whole affair was very impressive.

One of Stuart's gunners, George Neese, wrote of the young major general that day: "He was superbly mounted and his side arms gleamed in the morning sun like burnished silver. A long black ostrich plume waved gracefully from a black slouch hat cocked up on one side, held with a golden clasp. . . . He is the prettiest and most graceful rider I ever saw. I could not help but notice with what natural ease and comely elegance he sat his steed as it bounded over the field . . . he and his horse appear to be one and the same machine." Gunner Neese thought it all was "one grand magnificent pageant, inspiring enough to make even an old woman feel fightish."

The climax of the review came at the end when, in a sham battle, the cavalry charged the artillery. Many young ladies in the audience fashionably swooned into the arms of their gallant escorts as the yelling, saber-brandishing cavalrymen came thundering by.

Several days later, when General Lee could be present, another review was staged. This one was far more conservative and businesslike and, at General Lee's request, less wearing to horses, riders, and artillerymen alike. There were no charges, no sham battles. Nevertheless the first review had made its impression and when a real cavalry engagement took place not far from the scene of the mock one, the local citizenry was highly critical of the fact that the real one had not been won half so easily as the pretend one.

There was much criticism of Stuart in the Southern press, too. It was said that if he had not spent so much time holding fancy riding exhibits before the ladies and frequently dancing half the night, he would not have been taken by surprise by the almost successful Federal attack.

And it must be admitted that the Union cavalry did take Stuart by surprise. On the day after the review for General Lee, June 8, General Pleasonton and his blue cavalry bivouacked on the north bank of the Rappahannock—quietly, and without campfires. The Confederates were blissfully unaware the Federals were anywhere in the vicinity.

Indeed, they themselves were making plans to cross the Rappahannock in the opposite direction. Lee had asked Stuart to cross the next day, June 9, to protect the Confederate troops starting the northward movement that would eventually take them to Gettysburg. The brigades of cavalry, preparing to move out early in the morning, had encamped not far from the river. Stuart himself spent the night of June 8 in his bedroll on Fleetwood Hill. Almost the highest ground in the area, it commanded the open plains on three sides of it. Jeb had had his headquarters here for some time. Now he, too, was prepared to move out; his camp equipment was already packed and ready to go early the next morning.

Someone else was ready to go the next morning, too. At dawn the 8th New York Cavalry began to cross the Rappahannock. The startled Confederate pickets leaped into action, though they knew they were fighting against hopeless odds. Another group of about a hundred men under Major C. E. Flournoy hurried up to help the pickets. Meanwhile the Stuart Horse Artillery was in a dangerous position—only Major Flournoy's little group stood between them and the enemy. The artillerymen stopped where they were and set up two guns on the road. Under their protecting fire the rest of the battalion hurried back to set up guns in a better position farther to the rear.

As the battalions set up the guns General "Grumble" Jones, bareheaded, barefooted, and coatless, galloped into action at the head of his hurriedly half-dressed troops. Many of them had not even had time to saddle their horses. The skirmishing by these first two regiments to reach the enemy gave the rest of the cavalry precious time in which to get organized. As the fighting spread, Jones took a position to the left of the little St. James Church in the area and Wade Hampton formed four of his regiments into a line on the right. W. H. F. Lee, hurrying forward when he heard gunfire, set up his artillery on a nearby hill and put his dismounted men behind a stone fence in front of the hill. Attacks and counterattacks sent the blue and gray lines swaying back and forth across the area. Colonel M. C. Butler and his regiment were ordered out to protect the Confederate rear and set out to intercept a large group of Federals moving in from Kelly's Ford. This Union force split. Butler placed his troops before one column, but General Robertson, who should have stopped the other, unaccountably did not oppose them.

Because the fighting was ranging over such a widespread area, Stuart sent his adjutant, Major H. B. McClellan, to Fleetwood Hill. This area would be used as a headquarters. All the various Confederate brigades and regiments were to report their movements to that location and get further orders. Jeb himself galloped off toward St. James Church, where the fighting was at its fiercest.

There was not a bit of camp left set up on Fleetwood. Major McClellan and his couriers were its only occupants. Near the foot of the hill was a small howitzer that had been moved back from the fighting at the river when it ran out

of ammunition. Little did anyone suspect the vital role it
was to play!

About two hours after Jeb had set out for the front lines
a lone scout came tearing up Fleetwood Hill. Breathlessly
he told Major McClellan that the enemy was marching up
from Kelly's Ford and approaching the Confederate rear
in force—and unopposed. McClellan could not believe it—
General Robertson's brigade had been ordered out to prevent just such a maneuver! He sent the scout back to check
again—surely it must be Confederate troops coming. In less
than five minutes the scout was back. "There," he said,
pointing, "you can see for yourself!" Sure enough, in the
distance could be seen a long blue column filling the road
and rapidly approaching nearby Brandy Station. In no
time at all they would be at Fleetwood Hill. The center of
the entire Confederate communication setup was in danger.

Major McClellan leaped into action. A feverish search
through an old limber chest nearby brought to light a few
defective shells and round shot. Quickly the howitzer was
hauled up the hill. Slow firing was started. Major McClellan
sent out one courier after another—maybe *one* could get
through to tell General Stuart of the dangerous situation. If
the Federals should capture Fleetwood Hill, they could
entrench their artillery and command the whole area!

Meanwhile the Union forces were surprised suddenly to
receive artillery fire just as they emerged from the woods.
They had not met any opposition since they had crossed
the river. "Aha," they said, "so *this* is where the Confederates are set up in force!" As a matter of fact only Major
McClellan and the little howitzer crew remained on the
hill—even the last courier had been sent for help. The Federal troops, unaware of this, halted and began to organize for

a serious attack, setting up three guns to shell the hill in the meantime.

By now McClellan's couriers were beginning to reach Stuart. The young general's reaction to the first courier was like McClellan's. "Ride back there and see what all that foolishness is about," he ordered testily. The second courier galloped up to the sound of cannon fire, however—there could be no doubt of the report this time!

Immediately Jeb ordered the nearest troops—a mile and a half away—to Fleetwood. To Major McClellan and the perspiring gun crew on the hill the minutes of waiting seemed like hours. Then, just as the howitzer was firing its last shell, gray horsemen could be seen trotting up the hillside. McClellan dashed down to urge them forward. They had come in such haste, there had been no time even to form into squadrons or platoons. In contrast the 1st New Jersey Cavalry was simultaneously moving up the other side of the hill in what Major McClellan described as "magnificent order, in columns of squadrons, with flags and guidons flying." The two groups clashed at the top of the hill before the unorganized Confederates had time to do anything more than speed up to a gallop.

A few minutes later Stuart himself thundered up. He had ordered Hampton and Jones to leave the St. James Church area and bring their troops to Fleetwood Hill where they soon arrived. Now began a fierce battle for this key position. Charges and countercharges swept back and forth across the area. The shock of horseman riding into horseman and saber ringing against saber filled the air as the troops locked in desperate hand-to-hand fighting. Both sides showed great bravery and daring.

It was a charge by a part of Wade Hampton's brigade

that turned the tide. One eyewitness said, "This charge was as gallantly made and gallantly met as any the writer ever witnessed during nearly four years of active service. . . . As the blue and gray riders mixed in the smoke and dust of that eventful charge, minutes seemed to elapse before . . . the intermixed and disorganized mass began to recede, and we saw that the field was won to the Confederates."

The Confederate artillery was now able to move up the hill and open up on the retreating enemy. So much dust

and smoke hung over the area that, in the fighting that followed, it was hard to tell friend from foe even close at hand. One Federal colonel afterward reported picking up a Virginia trooper who said, "I can't tell you Yanks from our folks."

That was the end of the Union attack on Fleetwood Hill. The blue division reformed on the same ground it had originally formed on before the attack. Major McClellan said this part of the enemy "had been outnumbered and overpowered, but when the fighting was over he retired from the field at his own gait."

Meanwhile General "Rooney" Lee, whose forces had been left alone at St. James Church after Hampton and Jones had gone to Fleetwood, had been hard pressed and was badly wounded in the heavy fighting that followed. Finally the various divisions of Union cavalry were reunited. General Pleasonton, having found out what he wanted to—that there was Confederate infantry behind Stuart—decided to recross the Rappahannock. The exhausted Confederates made no real attempt to interfere. That night when Stuart got ready to set up his headquarters on Fleetwood Hill to show he had retained the ground and won what he felt was a brilliant victory, he was unable to. There was no room. The ground was covered with dead.

In this engagement—the greatest cavalry clash of the war and one of the greatest cavalry fights of the nineteenth century—Stuart had fought brilliant young Union cavalry commanders who were just beginning to come into their own. Using about 7000 men against Pleasonton's 10,000, he had lost 500 men to the Federals' 900. It had been a hard-fought and costly battle, however, and his critics in the

South blazed out against him for the narrow escape.

In one respect the Union cavalry profited from this engagement—it gave a tremendous boost to their morale. Before this they had been admittedly unequal to the excellent Southern cavalry. Their new-found ability to give the gray horsemen such a hard-fought battle as they had at Brandy Station gave them a confidence in their commanders and themselves that they had never had before. They felt that now they would be able to stand up even to Jeb Stuart!

Chapter XII.

GETTYSBURG

With the harsh criticism of his close shave at Brandy Station still ringing in his ears, praise-loving Jeb no doubt said to himself, "I'll show them!" Though the next few weeks brought much difficult fighting, they offered little opportunity for glory or honor for either the Confederate cavalry or their commander. Once again they were given the hard and thankless task of guarding the Blue Ridge Mountain passes.

Robert E. Lee was moving his army northward toward Pennsylvania and it was the cavalry's job to screen their advance. There was fierce fighting between the Union and Confederate cavalry in the mountain gaps around Aldie, Middleburg, and Upperville. Stuart and his men found that the great improvement in the blue cavalry noted at Brandy Station was no flash in the pan; they would never again be the easy mark they had been in the early months of the war. Both sides led fierce and valiant charges and were repulsed by fierce and valiant charges in these bloody battles in the Blue Ridge passes. It was here that Major Heros Von Borcke was wounded. He was never able to return to service in the field and Stuart missed him sorely, both personally and professionally.

It was at this time that John Mosby, "the Gray Ghost," brought his good friend Jeb Stuart news. Mosby and his "partisan rangers" (they would probably be called guerrillas today) spent a large part of their time behind enemy lines and often brought Stuart reports of enemy movements. Now the slender scout told Jeb that Hooker's Union Army was spread out so that a thrust up the middle could separate its wings and break its communications with Washington. Such an attack would also harass Hooker and divert his attention from Lee's northward move.

Jeb's blue eyes gleamed as he sat stroking his beard and listening to Mosby—here was an opportunity for another spectacular raid into enemy territory! The young major general at once sent word of this scheme to Lee, asking his permission to conduct an expedition along those lines.

General Lee's strategy called for Stuart to cover General Early's right flank on the march to Pennsylvania. Since it looked as though Stuart should be able to join Early just as easily taking the route Mosby suggested as that of the rest of the army, Lee gave his permission. He sent a detailed letter of instructions to his young cavalry commander.

It was a stormy, rainy night when the letter arrived. The cavalrymen were bivouacked in the open. There was an old house nearby where Jeb could have spent the night quite comfortably on the porch. This he refused to do. Wrapped in his oilcloth, he lay on the ground.

Major McClellan, his adjutant, had set up headquarters on the porch so he could read the night dispatches by candle as they came in. He tried to get Stuart to join him and told the young general he was subjecting himself to "needless exposure."

Jeb replied, "No. My men are exposed to this rain, and I will not fare any better than they."

During the night a courier brought the letter from General Lee. McClellan hated to wake Stuart but the letter was marked "Confidential" and a glance at its contents made him realize its importance. He found Stuart and read it to him. Stuart listened, then, wrapping his oilcloth closer, turned over and went back to sleep instantly, soaking rain nothwithstanding. Lee's letter gave Jeb the permission he wanted, telling him to get in touch with General Early at York, Pennsylvania, should he decide to use a route to the rear of the enemy. The final decision as to what he would or would not do the commanding general left with Stuart.

Lee had requested that two cavalry brigades be left behind to guard the Blue Ridge gaps and the rear of the Confederate Army as it moved north. Jeb left the troops of General Beverly Robertson and General "Grumble" Jones. These were the two commanders he liked least, though he considered "Grumble" efficient. He took with him the brigades of Wade Hampton, Fitz Lee, and "Rooney" Lee (commanded by Colonel Chambliss—"Rooney" was still recovering from the wound he had received at Brandy Station). Jeb has been criticized for leaving behind as the senior in command so poor an officer as General Robertson, but he took the men of the two Lees and Hampton—an excellent fighting team—as the best part of his corps to do what he considered the most important and difficult job.

On the dark night of June 25 the three brigades set out. Almost at once they found that General Hooker's army was already on the move. Jeb sent General R. E. Lee word of this but, as it never was delivered, Lee knew of neither this movement nor the change it made necessary in Stuart's plans. With Hooker's troops using the very route he himself had intended to use, Jeb decided to swing southward and move around the rear of the Union forces. True, this put the cavalry between Hooker's army and Washington, but it also put the whole of Hooker's army between Stuart and the rest of Lee's army.

The cavalry was traveling at a much slower pace than usual. No supply wagons traveled with the expedition and the gaunt, hungry horses had to be allowed time to graze. Crossing the Potomac delayed them still further. The deep and raging waters made this so hazardous that Major Mc-Clellan regarded their getting across at all as one of their most difficult accomplishments.

The men had to empty the chests and carry the ammunition by hand. The artillery pieces, though completely submerged the whole distance, were dragged across safely. The men, riding through swift waters that covered their saddles, sighed with relief as they struggled ashore. By 3 A.M. the whole column stood safely on the soil of Maryland.

After a short rest they moved on to Rockville, less than twenty miles from Washington. There they were busily cutting telegraph communications and gathering supplies when they got word that a long line of supply wagons was leaving the capital. Its destination was the Union Army of the Potomac, which had switched commanders once more—General Meade had replaced General Hooker. A handful of men from Hampton's brigade rushed out and captured the entire wagon train, turning back within sight of the defenses of Washington some that attempted to escape. The 125 wagons and all their animals had the newest and best equipment. It seemed a real prize at the time.

These wagons were to be a subject of much controversy later. Though they slowed the march of the cavalry tre-

mendously, Stuart refused to abandon them. Major Mc-
Clellan pointed out that, had Gettysburg been won instead
of lost, ". . . the persistency with which Stuart held on
to these wagons, and the difficulties he surmounted in
transporting them safely through an enemy's country during the next three days and nights of incessant marching
and fighting, would have been the cause of congratula-
tion." As it turned out, keeping the wagons added another
error in judgment to the score his critics charged up against
Stuart in his part in the Gettysburg campaign.

While Jeb was busily engaged in issuing paroles to Federal prisoners in Rockville—a slow process and another delay—Fitz Lee and his men were tearing up the track of the
Baltimore and Ohio Railroad, burning a bridge, and destroying telegraph lines. Meade's communications with
Washington were thus cut.

The column spent the night strung out the eight or so
miles from Westminster to Union Mills and there learned
that Kilpatrick's Federal cavalry was encamped only seven
miles away. Already the wagons were proving an en-
cumbrance. Without them the Confederates could have
quickly marched the ten miles to Hanover and entrenched
before Kilpatrick arrived. As it was, Kilpatrick got there
first. On June 30 a detachment of North Carolinians from
the head of Stuart's column entered Hanover and struck
the enemy. With support they could perhaps have completely routed the Federals, but after their first success they
were swept back as new blue reinforcements moved forward. The 125 wagons separated the advance guard of
Stuart's column from the rear and so no large force could
be hurried forward to the Carolinians' aid.

Jeb and his staff had been observing the Hanover fighting

from a nearby hill. When the Confederates were forced back, some of them turned and started to retreat. Jeb, after trying in vain to rally the men, stood his ground as the enemy came down the road in pursuit and fired his pistol at them. In a few minutes he and his staff found themselves in grave personal danger. The enemy held the road and the only other route of escape was cut by a deep ditch. The steep walls of the ditch were four feet high and the distance between them some ten to fifteen feet. Here was a real test of horse and horsemanship! It was a formidable obstacle, but to leap over it was the Confederates' only hope. Stuart, astride his favorite mare, Virginia, took off at a running leap. He sailed across easily and gracefully and landed on the other side with several feet to spare. Even in this moment of danger, Captain Blackford was struck by the superb horsemanship of his handsome young major general. He said in admiration, "I shall never forget the glimpse I then saw of this beautiful animal away up in mid-air over the chasm and Stuart's fine figure sitting erect and firm in the saddle." Some of the staff landed in the ditch and had a mad scramble climbing out, but somehow or other all escaped. Their pursuers stopped at the ditch.

That night Stuart started his column toward York. He wanted to find out if the Confederate Army was still to meet there. He had already been out of touch with them for five days.

Then began another nightmare march. Over 400 prisoners had been accumulated and they, plus the 125 wagons, made the long column drag along at an unbearably slow pace. Throughout the night there were constant stops as one wagon driver or another fell asleep through sheer exhaustion; when his wagon stopped, everything behind it stopped too. Men fell from their saddles into the road, asleep. Stuart wrote later: "Whole regiments slept in the saddle, their faithful animals keeping the road unguided." It took every effort of every member of Stuart's staff to keep the weary column moving. When the expedition reached Dover the next morning, Jeb sent out scouts to get information as to the whereabouts of the Confederate Army. Meanwhile he pushed on toward Carlisle, where he hoped to meet Ewell's troops. He found the enemy there instead. The gray infantrymen had left Carlisle long since.

Stuart drew his weary men into position and gave the Federal commander a choice. He could either surrender or evacuate the women and children to protect them from the shelling that would follow if he refused. General W. F. ("Baldy") Smith replied, "If you want the city, come and take it."

The exhausted Confederates started a slow bombardment. Men had to be shaken awake and orders shouted in their ears to get them to move. Many of them could not remember afterward whether they had actually shelled the city or only threatened to.

While the firing was going on, one of the couriers Jeb had sent out from Dover arrived triumphantly—he had found the army! He also brought orders for the cavalry to advance to Gettysburg at once. General Lee's forces had already been fighting there all day. Immediately Stuart stopped his attack on Carlisle and started south toward Gettysburg. It was one o'clock in the morning when they left and their goal was thirty miles away.

When Jeb ordered another all-night ride, his officers told him that if the exhausted men marched they would be in no condition to fight when they arrived. And the tireless

Jeb gave permission for a short halt. He himself stopped only for an hour, drawing his cape around him and leaning against a tree. Then he mounted again "as fresh, apparently," marveled John Esten Cooke, "as if he had slumbered from sunset to dawn."

The cavalry moved as fast as it could in its condition. It was on the afternoon of July 2, the second day of the bloody fighting at Gettysburg, that they once more rejoined the Army of Northern Virginia. They had been on the march for eight days and nights, most of the time in constant danger of attack by the enemy. At last they were again in the refuge of their own army. They sighed with relief and gratitude.

There are no detailed eyewitness accounts of Stuart's meeting with General Lee after these eight days of silence. It was reported a painful thing to see, though traditionally General Lee's only words were a quiet "Well, General Stuart, you are here at last."

If Jeb was hurt at his unenthusiastic reception, he did not show it. He got right to work. He found the commanding position he wanted on Cress Hill and on July 3 the cavalry took up its position on the Confederate left. A wood nearby helped hide them from the enemy. A stone dairy and Rummel's barn, a frame building, were close. Jeb fired a gun, apparently to tell General Lee he was now in position to the army's left. The signal also told the Federals where he was and accurate enemy fire descended on the Confederates at once. Dismounted Union cavalrymen moved in to attack the dismounted gray troopers Jeb had placed near Rummel's barn. Soon the open plain below Cress Ridge swarmed with men wielding saber and pistol and grappling hand to hand. In this fierce fighting, Wade Hampton fell with a fearful head wound. At last the Federal attack was halted and both sides returned to their original positions.

As twilight crept over the ridge the weary Confederates, already outnumbered and with no reserves at all, saw a whole blue brigade, unused till now, come up ready to move into action when the battle was resumed.

That day the Confederate infantry had suffered fearfully. Pickett's famous charge up Cemetery Ridge had been repulsed at terrible loss. Jeb first learned of the defeat when he visited the commanding general's headquarters late that night. Lee said sadly that the Confederates would not attack the next day. Stuart's position on Cress Ridge was now isolated. He withdrew his men in the darkness and rejoined the main army.

The Federals did not attack the next day. There was not even an artillery salute to the Fourth of July from their crippled batteries. The ground between the two enemies was covered with the dying and the dead.

Despite their hazardous position there seemed no sense of defeat in the Confederate lines. Nevertheless, food, ammunition, and all other supplies were running dangerously low and General Lee ordered a retreat that night. Ahead lay a long march through enemy territory, complicated by over 4000 prisoners and a wagon train fifteen miles long.

The cavalry guarded both flanks of the retreating gray army. Jeb commanded the worn and weary cavalrymen on one flank and Fitz Lee the other, and both met the enemy in numerous engagements before the Potomac was reached.

The fords of the river had disappeared when the Confederates reached its flooded banks. The Northerners rejoiced—here was Lee caught between the swollen river and Meade's whole army—surely he would not escape this time!

From July 8 to July 12, Stuart guarded the Confederate front and fended off attacks on the supply wagons. He and his men fought the Union cavalry of Buford and Kilpatrick daily—and fiercely.

Their personal hardships during this period included more than the dangers of battle. The men had been issued starvation rations, but the officers none at all. Fighting had swept the countryside bare of food supplies and they could buy none. If it had not been for the kindness of the daughter of a Confederate sympathizer who brought them food after dark for four or five days, Jeb and his staff would have suffered greatly from hunger.

Lack of rest was another punishment. For nearly two weeks the men had been in the saddle almost constantly. They were in a state of exhaustion. Even Jeb's iron endurance was sorely taxed. He fell asleep while waiting to eat or while waiting to sign McClellan's dispatches.

Both sides claimed the victory in these daily battles, and apparently each sincerely thought he had won the victory. Jeb's reported losses were heavier, but he accomplished his mission; Lee was able to select his position and fortify it while he waited for the floodwaters to recede. When the Federal Army advanced on July 12, they found the Confederate position too strong to attack.

At last the Potomac was fordable and on the night of July 13 Lee moved his army across to Virginia. The cavalry as usual had the dangerous task of bringing up the rear. Then, early on the morning of the fourteenth, after several skirmishes but no real difficulty, they, too, crossed. Instead of being crushed against the river and destroyed as the Northerners had hoped and confidently expected, Lee and his entire army had slipped safely back onto Virginia soil.

The part Jeb played—or did not play—in the Gettysburg campaign has been argued back and forth countless times. The absence of the cavalry, along with the slowness of Longstreet and Ewell in attacking and the failure of the Confederate forces to coordinate enough to act as an effective unit, are considered by many to have caused the defeat at Gettysburg. Jeb's delay did not actually deprive Lee of the use of cavalry, "the eyes and ears of the army"—the two brigades Stuart had left behind remained in daily contact with the commanding general. Lee did not request information from Robertson, however, nor did Robertson volunteer to get any. Major McClellan said, "It was not the want of cavalry that General Lee bewailed, for he had enough of it had it been properly used. It was the absence of Stuart himself that he felt so keenly; for on him he had learned to rely to such an extent that it seemed as if his cavalry were concentrated in his person, and from him alone could information be expected."

Though Jeb was perhaps unwise and made some errors of judgment on his long raid, he did not disobey his orders from Lee, as some critics have charged. His orders left the decision as to his course of action up to him and he stayed within the latitude given him. Lee himself never said otherwise.

Meanwhile his presence in an area apart from the main army made it necessary for the Federals to divert troops in his direction and caused confusion as to just what the Confederates planned and where they were going.

Whether Stuart's arrival at Gettysburg two days earlier would have made a difference or not no one can definitely say. His part in that defeat must remain a historical controversy.

Chapter XIII.

HIDE-AND-SEEK

IN THE little breather the cavalry enjoyed after Gettysburg, Stuart worked on reorganizing his corps. He sought promotions for men like Wade Hampton and Fitz Lee and he also asked that the troublesome and inefficient Beverly Robertson be removed from his command. General Lee agreed to all three requests.

During this breather trouble broke out again between Stuart and "Grumble" Jones. Jones did not get promoted and he blamed Stuart. After an angry argument in which Jones evidently cursed Stuart bitterly, he was court-martialed for insubordination. General Lee felt that the personal antagonism between the two men made it wise to transfer Jones, whom he still considered an able officer, and he did so.

The winter of 1863–64 was one of hardship and privation for the Confederates. Jeb's men lacked food and clothing. Their dwindling number of horses also endured almost constant hunger. The whole Confederate Army suffered from these shortages but learned to get by on surprisingly little. Their high morale and cheerfulness were amazing under the circumstances. There was some singing at the cavalry headquarters that winter, but much less than usual—Sweeney had died of pneumonia and his gay banjo no longer rang around the campfires.

During his off-duty hours Jeb spent much of his time writing to his beloved Flora. They were expecting a child that winter and his letters to her were especially sweet and thoughtful. When the baby came—a little girl—she was called Virginia Pelham Stuart, two names dear to her father's heart: one of his native state and one of his lost friend.

On October 9, 1863, the very day Virginia Pelham was born, General Lee began to move his army around the right flank of Meade's Union forces in Culpeper County. Thus began what is called the Bristoe campaign. Once more Jeb and his men had the job of protecting and concealing the infantry's movements. Once more they engaged in almost daily skirmishing with the enemy.

They even met the Federal cavalry again on their old battleground at Brandy Station. This time the Federals got to Fleetwood Hill first. As in the previous battle there, both sides fought fiercely. Three Virginia regiments each made five separate and distinct saber charges over the familiar battlefield, now bloody once more. The Federals were finally pushed back until they were all on Fleetwood Hill. Stuart declined to attack such a strong position. When Fitz Lee moved his division as though he were going to cut the enemy off from the river, the Federal cavalry, skillfully protected by their artillery, withdrew and crossed the river that night. Again a worn and battle-weary Confederate cavalry bivouacked near Brandy Station, feeling they had won a hard-fought victory.

The next morning Stuart and most of his command set out to cover the infantry's movement toward Bristoe as Lee still maneuvered to flank Meade. Jeb left Colonels Rosser and Young and a small force near Fleetwood as pickets. That same afternoon three corps of Federal infantry and a division of cavalry started moving toward Culpeper in search of Lee. They ran into Rosser, who could of course only fall back before such numbers. Colonel Young moved his men up and the two groups fired together so effectively that the Federals thought they were a large force and decided not to attack.

That night was an uneasy one for the far outnumbered Confederates. Not knowing what the morning might bring, Rosser and Young decided to make their limited force seem as formidable as possible. Campfires were lighted at every possible point—a whole division could have warmed its hands at them. Colonel Young's command happened to have the regimental band with it and the musicians were sent scurrying from one place to another to play their stirring airs. One would have thought there were numerous bands, each one trying to outdo the other as it serenaded its own "regiment."

During the night General Meade discovered Lee was not at Culpeper after all. He recalled his troops from that area and sent them hurrying off toward the Orange and Alexandria Railroad. When morning came the Confederates were happy indeed to find themselves no longer facing the overwhelming numbers of bluecoats. The strategy of Rosser and Young had made the enemy move much more cautiously than he needed to and had perhaps averted what would have been a very costly fight for the Confederates.

On October 13, Lee asked Stuart to reconnoiter the blue

forces in the vicinity of Catlett's Station on the Orange and
Alexandria Railroad. Jeb set out at once. Lee's army was
near Warrenton and some Federal troops had been sighted
at Warrenton Junction, only nine miles farther down the
railroad. Between these two locations lay Auburn and Catlett's Station.

Jeb led his troops through the tiny hamlet of Auburn
and, as a precaution, decided to leave Lomax and his brigade
there. The main body of cavalry then moved on. Coming
suddenly out of the woods, they found themselves at a
vantage point from which they could look down on both
Catlett's Station and Warrenton Junction. Surprise turned
Jeb's eyes to blue fire. Here was no mere handful of Federals—spread below him along the railroad were thousands
and thousands of bluecoats—undoubtedly most, or maybe
even all, of Meade's army! Infantry, artillery, and huge
numbers of wagon trains filled the eye—all hurrying northward, streaming along in solid columns.

If only Lee could move down quickly that night and
catch the Federals on the march, Jeb thought. He sent
Major Venable, one of his staff officers, to let the commanding general know at once of this wonderful opportunity. Meanwhile the cavalry would have to lie low if the
element of surprise were to be retained until Lee could
bring up a force large enough to be effective.

Then came another surprise. Major Venable sent back
word that Auburn was now in the hands of the enemy but
that he was sure he could detour and still reach Lee. This
was an unpleasant piece of information. Stuart and his men
were now between two large groups of Federals. Here was
a quick turnabout—instead of hoping for a surprise attack
against the Union troopers, the Confederates would need

all sorts of ingenuity and luck to escape meeting them! Jeb and his men were in an area about five miles square almost completely surrounded by the converging lines of the marching enemy.

Obviously there was no easy way out. The only thing to do was to find a place to hide until the enemy had gone by. And hiding horses, men, seven artillery pieces, ordnance wagons, and ambulances was no simple matter! Jeb began a careful search for a hiding place. Luck was with him; almost in sight of Auburn itself they found a little valley. It had a narrow entrance concealed by woods, and widened as it extended back from the thoroughfare.

Quickly men and wagons were hustled into the little valley. "As if by magic," said Major McClellan, "the road was cleared of horsemen, artillery, and wagons, and darkness found us snugly sheltered beneath the hills which raised their friendly crests between us and danger. How thankful we were for those hills! How thankful for that darkness!"

The guns were quickly rolled into place on the crest of the hill, only about three hundred yards from the road down which the enemy was passing. Pickets were hidden in bushes near the valley entrance. Everything possible had been done. All they could do now was wait, watchful and quiet.

Keeping the men quiet was no problem. Every man there understood how dangerous his situation was and how imperative it was that he be silent. Unfortunately the mules did not have this same grasp of the situation. Hungry and tired, they constantly brayed their unhappiness to the world at the tops of their voices. Finally Jeb stationed a man at the head of every ordnance mule team to try to keep the animals quiet. Even with this precaution, they still sounded

forth every once in a while, making Confederate hearts
quake each time.

Fortunately the enemy was making a good bit of noise
too. Jeb and his men could hear the sound of Union officers
giving orders. They could even distinguish the difference
between the noises of the artillery wheels rolling by and the
supply wagons.

During the anxious night Stuart and his staff discussed
all sorts of plans of action. Jeb even suggested the possibility of turning off the leader of one of the wagon trains
as though by order of a superior, and then taking his place
with his own command and marching along in the Federal
column in the darkness until they reached a safe place. The
staff thought this might work with a small group, but was
too dangerous to try with two brigades.

During that endless night Stuart sent six couriers to
Robert E. Lee; one at a time. Their only hope seemed to
lie in help from him, or in the possibility that the Federals
would have passed their hideaway by daylight. Few of the
Confederates could close their eyes that night, but Jeb,
using Blackford's stomach for a pillow, slept like a log.

Dawn finally came. Through the trees Jeb could see a
group of Union soldiers who had halted close by to fix their
breakfast. The Confederates watched the Federals lighting
their fires, getting out their coffeepots—they thought they
could even smell the coffee. Soon some of the bluejackets
started hunting for a spring. In a few minutes more a clash
would be inevitable.

Quickly Jeb ordered the cannon loaded and quietly rolled
forward. Every man got his weapons ready. Unless General Lee's help arrived very quickly, they would soon be
engaged in fighting as desperate as any they had ever

known. Then, just at that tense moment, distant rifle fire sounded sharply in the morning air. It came from the direction of Warrenton! At last relief was on the way!

This was the only signal Jeb needed. "Fire!" he shouted. Confederate cannon roared out. Coffeepots leaped high and surprised Union soldiers jumped for cover. In a few minutes a blue battle line had formed and started forward. The Confederate horse artillery fired with all its might and the dismounted cavalry fought with the skill of seasoned infantrymen. If they noticed what Jeb's discerning ear caught at once—that the supporting Confederate fire in the distance had already stopped—they did not indicate it. In a few minutes the Federal line broke and fled under the hot shelling.

Stuart knew another attack would come in minutes and his guns must be moved or lost. Quickly he sent forward the veteran 1st Carolina Regiment in a charge to cover the withdrawal of the artillery. In the confusion that followed, the young major general saw a chance for their salvation. A quick gallop in a half circle around the Federal flank might take them out of danger.

Hurriedly everything was made ready. Artillery, ambulances, wagons—all were prepared to take off at the instant of command. Every man sat in his saddle, tense and ready to dash forward. Suddenly Jeb waved his saber and shouted the order. Down raced the troopers, guns and wagons rattling along behind them. Around the Union flank they galloped furiously—the Federals hardly made an attempt to stop them. Many a sigh of relief was breathed in the Confederate ranks—now all it would take to get back to the shelter of Robert E. Lee's army was a more or less routine ride.

The fight at Bristoe Station ended Lee's advance, and Stuart and the cavalry followed and harassed the retiring Union troops for three days. On the fourth day, October 18, Jeb and Fitz Lee moved back not far from Warrenton. That evening Stuart was attacked with such vigor that he thought the whole enemy cavalry was going to engage the division he was leading personally.

He withdrew to the southern bank of the Broad Run at Buckland. There he hoped to hold off the enemy until Fitz Lee could join him. Meanwhile Fitz sent a plan: "You fall back across the stream and lure the enemy on; at a given signal you fall on their front and I will attack their flank at the same time."

"Agreed," said Stuart. The attack went just as planned. Jeb withdrew; then, when the Union troops followed, he suddenly turned and attacked. The surprised Federals halted in confusion. Then, understanding they had ridden into an ambush, they wheeled around and raced off. For five miles the gray cavalry galloped after them.

The superior physical condition of the Federal horses enabled them to get away before the poorly mounted Confederates could inflict serious damage. Nevertheless the gray cavalry did make some captures. Stuart bewailed the fact that "We got only 250 prisoners and eight or ten ambulances!" Jeb and his men had found the whole mad dash behind the fleeing bluejackets an exhilarating experience. Ever after they referred to this engagement as the "Buckland Races."

Chapter XIV.

FATEFUL DAY
AT YELLOW TAVERN

Early 1864 found the Confederates' supply situation growing even worse. Effective guns and ammunition were getting harder to find. The Army of Northern Virginia continued to suffer dreadfully from cold, lack of food and clothing. Starvation of both men and animals seemed a very real and constant possibility. Food and clothes sent from home were probably the only things that enabled the men and officers to endure that terrible winter.

During a lull in the fighting Flora came to Orange Court House for a visit. Their new baby daughter, Virginia Pelham, was a great comfort and joy to Jeb and his wife after the loss of little Flora, and others enjoyed the presence of the baby too. General Lee was among the many visitors who called on "Miss Virginia."

Jeb made occasional trips to Richmond during this period and society hostesses in the capital fought for his presence at their balls and tableaux. He was a success wherever he went.

The city soon turned from gaiety to uneasiness, however. A Federal attack in the last days of winter found Kilpatrick leading about 3500 men toward Richmond. The force split in two and the advance column under Colonel Ulric Dahlgren moved off to try to free some of the captured Federals at the nearby Confederate prison before rejoining Kilpatrick for a joint attack on the capital.

A group of about 150 Confederates from the 9th Virginia Cavalry managed to ambush Dahlgren and his men— Dahlgren himself was killed in the first volley. Found on his body were official papers ordering that the city of Richmond be burned and destroyed and President Jefferson Davis and his Cabinet killed. Generals Meade and Kilpatrick later denied that these orders had been given by them, but it made little difference: the South was already aroused to renewed anger and patriotism by the "Dahlgren Papers."

The bloody Wilderness campaign got its start on May 4, 1864. The Federal forces taking part had yet another new commanding general. This one had been imported from the western theater where he had marked up an impressive series of victories. His name was Ulysses S. Grant.

Grant led his forces across the Rapidan and began a movement that he hoped would take him around the Confederate flank and put him between Lee and Richmond. Fitz Lee's division was thrown before the Union force to hold it until General Anderson could move Longstreet's corps up to Spotsylvania Court House. Fitz Lee's whole command fought dismounted. They wielded saber and pistol so stubbornly that they were able to hold back Grant's men until Anderson arrived. Then they moved back, fighting as they went, until they were directly in front of Anderson's concealed position. The Federals came charging forward, only to be surprised by the sudden appearance of the infantry. The bluecoats were driven back.

Soon thereafter Stuart himself galloped up with additional troops, both his own cavalry and more of Anderson's infantry. At Anderson's request, he acted as commander until the rest of the army arrived and the cavalry was relieved. During this period of several hours Major McClellan thought that "he exposed himself to fire with more than his usual disregard of danger. . . . I was the only member of his staff present. Not even a courier attended us. He kept me so busy in carrying messages to General Anderson, and some of these seemed so unimportant, that at last the thought occurred to me that he was endeavoring to shield me from danger. I said to him: 'General, my horse is weary. You are exposing yourself, and you are alone. Please let me remain with you.' He smiled at me kindly, but bade me go to General Anderson with another message."

The next day, May 9, a large force of artillery and about 12,000 cavalry led by Union General Philip Sheridan began a move toward Richmond. Within two hours Stuart's cavalry was on their trail. Following the enemy through Beaver Dam Station, Jeb grabbed a few seconds to gallop to the house where Flora and the children were visiting. Having found that they were safe, he leaned from the saddle to kiss them good-by and galloped off once more. It was the last time he saw them.

Back with his column, Jeb decided to split his forces. Gordon's brigade was to follow the enemy from the rear while Stuart and Fitz Lee's two brigades attempted to hurry forward and throw themselves between Richmond and the Federals. Stuart had hoped to ride through the night, but Lee's men were so exhausted that he had to let them rest.

He wanted them to start again promptly at 1 A.M. He called Major McClellan. "Don't close your eyes," he instructed, "until you see Fitz's whole command mounted and on the march at the appointed hour." When the troops left, McClellan went to Stuart and woke him and the staff. While they were getting ready, the adjutant lay down to try to snatch a minute's sleep. He said later, "The party rode off as I lay in a half-conscious condition, and I heard someone say: 'General, here's McClellan, fast asleep. Shall I wake him?'

" 'No,' he replied; 'he has been watching while we were asleep. Leave a courier with him, and tell him to come on when his nap is out.' "

McClellan said, "I gratefully accepted this unusual and unlooked-for interposition in my behalf. . . ." After his rest the adjutant hurried forward and caught up with the young general. They rode side by side and McClellan remembered that "we conversed on many matters of personal interest. He was more quiet than usual, softer, and more communicative. It seems now that the shadow of the near future was already upon him." They were on their way to Yellow Tavern.

They reached their destination about 10 A.M. Stuart was pleased to find they had beat the Federals there. He sent McClellan to Richmond to see if General Bragg had enough infantry to hold the trenches there so he would know where to place his cavalry. When McClellan got back to Yellow Tavern heavy fighting was already under way. About four that afternoon a brigade of Federal cavalry charged, attacking the whole gray line at once. As always, Stuart moved to the point of the greatest danger. He joined a group of men who were especially hard hit. One of the privates remembered his coming: "General Stuart came riding slowly through the woods, whistling and entirely alone." A captain who saw him also noted his whistling and mentioned he was "seemingly in a gay mood. . . ." Jeb calmly took a position between two privates. By his own courageous example he steadied the whole group as the enemy swept completely past them and then was driven back.

As the Federal tide receded, one man, running and on foot, turned and fired at the fine figure on the gray horse. Jeb clutched his side and slumped forward. The plumed hat fell to the ground. "General," cried one of the boys near him, "are you hit?" Captain Dorsey came running forward. He tried to lead the general's horse but couldn't calm the frightened animal. Finally he helped Jeb to the ground and propped him against a tree while he sent for another horse.

"Leave me, Dorsey, and go back to your men and fight," Stuart urged.

Captain Dorsey refused. "Sir," he said, "I can't obey that order; I can't leave until you are in a safe place."

Their present situation was certainly not a safe one—only a handful of men stood between the wounded general and the oncoming enemy. Finally the horse came and Jeb was lifted onto his back. Captain Dorsey reluctantly turned his wounded commander over to Private Wheatley while he went back to his men. Wheatley got an ambulance just as Fitz Lee dashed up and leaped off his gray mare. Stuart smiled at Fitz. "Go ahead, old fellow," he said, turning over his command to Lee. "I know you'll do what's right."

As the ambulance was being driven from the scene of action, Jeb saw his men retreating in confusion. Even though in great pain and shock from the wound in his abdomen, he pulled himself up on his elbow and shouted in something of his glorious ringing voice, "Go back! Go back and do your duty as I have done mine. I'd rather die than be whipped!"

Once the ambulance was under way, Dr. Fontaine and Lieutenant Hullihen turned the general so his wound could be examined.

"Honey-bun," said Stuart to Hullihen, calling him by his customary nickname, "how do I look in the face?"

"General," the lieutenant replied, "you are looking right well. You will be all right."

Jeb answered, "Well, I don't know how this will turn out; but if it is God's will that I shall die I am ready."

Dr. Fontaine's findings were not encouraging. The wound, in the abdomen and perhaps liver, was almost bound to be fatal. Knowing that Stuart must be in terrible pain, the doctor offered him some brandy to ease his suffering. Jeb refused. When he was twelve years old he had promised his mother he would not drink—he never had and he saw no reason to now.

The enemy held the turnpike, so the ambulance had to jolt over a detour to reach Richmond. Stuart suffered fearfully on the long rough ride. It was late that night before they reached the home of Dr. Charles Brewer, his brother-in-law. The day of May 11, 1864, had been a long one for Jeb Stuart.

The next day Jeb had several visitors. Von Borcke came, and Major McClellan. Flora and the children had started toward Richmond as soon as they received news of his wound but had not arrived. Jeb told McClellan to send his personal effects to Flora and talked to him about the disposition of his official papers. Then he said, "I wish you to take one of my horses and Venable the other." He asked,

"Which is the heavier rider?" McClellan said he thought Venable was. "Then," he said, "let Venable have the gray horse, and you take the bay."

He left his gold spurs to Mrs. Lily Lee, the widow of an old friend, and his sword to his son. Then his thoughts turned to the battlefield and he reminded McClellan that Fitz Lee might need him. As McClellan was leaving, President Jefferson Davis came in.

"General," he said, "how do you feel?"

"Easy," said Stuart, "but willing to die if God and my country think I have fulfilled my destiny and done my duty."

Later he requested the minister visiting him to sing "Rock of Ages." In a shadow of his normal voice he joined in. He asked for Flora several times that afternoon, but she had not come. Wanting so much to see her, he asked the doctor if he thought he could live through the night. The physician told him frankly there was little hope.

Jeb said, "I am resigned if it be God's will; but I would like to see my wife. But God's will be done." Later he murmured, "I am going fast now; I am resigned; God's will be done." That was the end. Flora did not arrive until three hours later.

When Robert E. Lee got news of Stuart's wound, he turned to the officers around him. "Gentlemen," he said, his voice shaking, "we have very bad news. General Stuart has been mortally wounded." He stood silent a few minutes. Then he added his great tribute: "He never brought me a piece of false information." When word came of Stuart's death, Lee said, "I can scarcely think of him without weeping."

Jeb Stuart's genius as a commander of light cavalry has been praised many times. His cold steadiness under fire, his clarity of thinking under great pressure, his ability to assess a battlefield situation instantly and accurately and then carry out his spontaneously conceived plan—all these set him apart as a field commander and account for his rapid rise in command and his lasting military reputation.

He also had an "unconquerable resolution," the same stick-to-it-tiveness he had shown in his boyhood encounter with the hornets and which he demonstrated time and again in his military career. He proved himself an intelligence officer of the first water and the only things in his career for which he has been criticized grew out of an excess of the boldness that characterized everything he did.

The commemorative order Fitz Lee issued to the Confederate cavalry contained a fitting tribute. He who had fought beside him so often said, "Stuart had no superior as a soldier. . . ."

BIBLIOGRAPHY

Blackford, W. W., *War Years with Jeb Stuart*. Charles Scribner's Sons, New York, 1945.

Cooke, John Esten, *Wearing of the Gray*. Indiana University Press, Bloomington, 1959 (reissue).

Davis, Burke, *Jeb Stuart, the Last Cavalier*. Rinehart and Company, New York, 1957.

Eggleston, George C., *A Rebel's Recollections*. Hurd and Houghton, New York, 1875.

Freeman, Douglas Southall, *Lee's Lieutenants*. 3 vols. Charles Scribner's Sons, New York, 1945.

Freeman, Douglas Southall, *Lee of Virginia*. Charles Scribner's Sons, New York, 1958.

Henry, Robert S., *The Story of the Confederacy*. Revised. Grosset and Dunlap, New York, 1931; Bobbs-Merrill, Indianapolis, 1936.

Jones, Virgil Carrington, *Gray Ghosts and Rebel Raiders*. Henry Holt, New York, 1956.

McClellan, H. B. *I Rode with Jeb Stuart: Life and Campaigns of Major-General J. E. B. Stuart*. Civil War Centennial Series, Indiana University Press, Bloomington, 1958.

Miers, Earl Schenck, *Billy Yank and Johnny Reb*. Rand McNally and Company, Skokie, Illinois, 1939.

Strode, Hudson, *Jefferson Davis, Confederate President*. Harcourt, Brace and Company, New York, 1959.

Thomason, John W. Jr., *Jeb Stuart*. Charles Scribner's Sons, New York, c. 1929.

Von Borcke, Heros, *Memoirs of the Confederate War for Independence*. 2 vols. Blackwood and Son, London, 1866.

Wiley, Bell I. *The Life of Johnny Reb*. Bobbs-Merrill Company, Indianapolis, 1943.

Warner, Ezra J., *Generals in Gray*. Louisiana State University Press, Baton Rouge, 1959.

Williamson, Mary L., *Life of J. E. B. Stuart*. B. F. Johnson Publishing Company, Richmond, 1914.

INDEX